To my dear sisters at ♡ the Carmel of the Incarn[...] ~

Except for His Wings

Michael Dodd

F

Do E

Pileated Press
5120 Brookside Drive - #300
Madison, WI 53718

Cover design by Tom Scharbach

ISBN-10: 1523874791
ISBN-13: 978-1523874798

Dedicated to the staff and patrons
of Kilbourn Public Library
in Wisconsin Dells
where this book was drafted during
National Novel Writing Month 2015

The town of Blakesfield, Texas, its residents and the events described in this volume are all fictions. Any resemblance to people, places and happenings is a most amazing and unintentional coincidence.

Alcoholics Anonymous and other programs based on the Twelve Steps are quite real and have helped many people find their way to a fuller and happier life. Some of the gems garnered from friends who found such help are scattered throughout this tale with all due respect.

May everyone be joyous, happy and free.

Run my dear,
from anything
That may not strengthen
Your precious budding wings.

Khwāja Shamsu ud-Dīn Muhammad Hāfez-e Shīrāzī

(1325 – 1389)

Chapter 1

"Except for his wings, Daddy, he looks like any other boy," Katie said between mouthfuls of turkey mole.

I scooped another drip of strained peaches from Billy Bob's chin and into his mouth.

"What, snookums?"

Katie had been rattling on for ten minutes, but Billy Bob had required my full attention up to this point. I had just nodded and "Um-hummed" my way through the recital. Had she said something about wings?

"Daddy! You're not listening!"

I had to admit she had me there. I put down the spoon and wiped Billy Bob's chin.

"Okay, sweetie. Who's the guy with the wings?"

"I told you, he's the new kid I saw at the park."

The park was a few blocks from our house. There was a playground with swings, a slide and what we used to call monkey bars in my own childhood. A large sandbox, a few benches, a broken drinking fountain and a grove of live oak trees completed the scene.

Our town was small and had limited resources. Peck's Park was the only place for the kids to play except for the school playground. That was surrounded by a high cyclone fence and the gate was locked as soon as the yellow school buses pulled away in the afternoon. Several of us parents had asked the school board to leave it open longer, but they muttered something about liability insurance and the gate remained locked after hours. It also remained locked all summer, meaning Peck's Park was the place where kids gathered to while away the hours.

Most of them came from families with as few resources as the town of Blakesfield. There was no industry, the farms had all dried up and blown away, the big pecan business my mother's family used to run had folded due to poor management and most folks worked at the large prison farm outside of town or not at all.

Blakesfield was too far from any big city for us to get decent television reception with antennas and too small for any cable company to string wires out our way. A handful of people had those ginormous satellite dishes that you used to see everywhere. Even the satellite dished in our part of Texas were bigger than elsewhere. Some people thought that was a reason to brag, but then, Texans will brag about anything, even if they have to make it up.

There was a small AM radio statio that played country music from the days when Tom T. Hall and Merle Haggard were big names. KKBF – Klassic Kountry Blakesfield, they called themselves. I won't tell you what the teenagers called it, but I think you can guess. Even the radio station shut down at eleven at night, but no one was up to listen to it anyway. There were no bars, no pool halls, no movies. Nothing for kids or adults. Why we were still there was a bit of a mystery. I recall something from school about a body at rest remaining at rest. I guess that was what most of us folks in Blakesfield did. We remained at rest, if rest is what it was.

"Okay, Katydid," I said, lifting Billy Bob out of his high chair where he had begun to nod after his peaches. "Come help me put your brother back in his crib and then you can tell me more about it."

Billy Bob is an easy baby to take care of, which is a good thing. After LuNella ran off with the typewriter repairman, I have been on my own with the kids.

Katie is eleven and a big help. She used to ask about her mama and when she was going to come back. One day I sat her down, handed her a Coke and told her the facts of life. Well, the facts of life insofar as they related to her mama, who was never coming back. She cried for an hour and a half while I held her and rocked her back and forth. Since that day, she has not mentioned her mama once. But not long after that tearful conversation, I saw her looking through the old box of photos we kept in the bottom drawer of the dresser in my bedroom. I suspected she went in there from time to time when I wasn't around, and some resentful part of me was tempted to throw those pictures away. But I wasn't quite angry enough with my ex-wife to do that. Not yet, anyway. It would just hurt Katie, and she hurt enough as it was.

We got Billy Bob cleaned up and settled down. He gurgled once and closed his eyes. A minute later he was asleep. I motioned to Katie to tiptoe and we left the room with exaggerated silence like characters in an old movie and went back to the kitchen.

"You want some iced tea?" I asked, opening the refrigerator door and peering inside. As usual, there was not a lot to see.

"No, thank you," she said, slipping onto the wobbly white chair where she always sat at the kitchen table.

I wanted a beer, but I couldn't afford to drink any more. Not because of money, of which I had plenty, but because … well, I couldn't. Wayne, my sponsor, keeps reminding me that there is no problem in life that drinking won't make worse for people like me. I sighed.

There had been a time when I thought there was no problem that drinking wouldn't make a whole lot better. A few visits to the county jail had changed my mind. I'm not saying that my drinking was why LuNella ran off with that typewriter salesman, but it sure didn't give her much reason to hang around with me.

There was still a bottle of Liberation Ale in the back of the refrigerator. It was an India Pale Ale from Live Oak Brewing in Austin. Someone gave me some last Christmas and it was so bitter that I hadn't finished it off before I quit drinking. To give you an idea of how bitter that had to be, I would drink just about anything as long as it had alcohol. I kept that bottle around, despite Wayne's advice, partly to prove I could choose not to drink it and partly to remind myself of how bitter drinking had made my life.

Wayne was not impressed by either of those reasons.

"As long as you think you have some power over alcohol, you haven't fully realized the depth of your problem, son. And all you have to do to be reminded of how bitter drinking made your life is to look at the empty side of the bed every night when you go to bed and get up in the morning. Or at that little girl and little boy of yours who are growing up without their mama."

Wayne could be brutally honest. Sometimes I thought it was just brutal. I figured he was right about the ale, but what the hell. I shoved the bottle into a corner and pushed salad dressing bottles in front of it. But I didn't toss it out. I wasn't ready to do that yet.

I pulled out the heavy glass tea pitcher and closed the refrigerator door.

I got one of the tall glasses out of the cabinet, one of the ones with a faded image of Fred Flintstone on it, and poured iced tea into it. I looked at Katie and cocked an eyebrow, but she shook her head. I put the pitcher back and found an old lemon in the crisper drawer, almost but not quite dried out.

"That lemon's nigh onto dry," my mama would have said. "There's not enough pucker in there to count."

I cut it in half and dropped both halves into the glass, stirred it around with my finger and sat down.

"So there's a new boy at the park," I said. "With wings?"

I tilted my head back and raised an eyebrow. I thought it made me look wise. Or sexy. Depending on what the situation called for. Wayne told me it just made me look like I was having a stroke.

See? Just brutal.

Katie nodded.

"Yep, wings. He just showed up today. He was wearing cargo pants, a red t-shirt and he's barefoot. And he has wings. Big white wings."

Chapter 2

I drank more of the tea and wished it had more bite. The lemon did have enough juice to pucker my mouth, but not enough to clear my head. I guess the new kid had some of those wings like the girls wear for Halloween and stuff. Sounded like he was asking for trouble if he was going to wear them around here. Central Texas was not known for tolerance of anything out of the ordinary. You know, things like Democrats and socialists and other low-lifes.

"Where's he from?" I asked.

"I don't know. He doesn't talk."

"Doesn't talk?"

"No, sir. He never said a word. When he first showed up, he just stood on the edge of the park and watched us for a long time. Then he came over and got on one of the swings and pushed himself back and forth, back and forth. It was cool, because you know how you push yourself back and up with your feet, to see how high you can go?"

I sipped at the glass, realized the tea was gone and fished out a lemon half. I put it in my mouth and bit down, making Katie wince. My mama taught me to eat lemons.

"Yeah," I said, after I had chewed the lemon up and swallowed it. I fished out the other half and put it in my mouth. Katie looked away.

"Anyway, he did that and he got higher and higher, and then he just started flapping those white wings and kept going up and up and up. We all stopped and watched, and I thought he was going to go over the top of the swing, but he quit and then just kind of floated back down with a grin."

"That must've been something," I said, wondering when Katie had started making up stories.

Was this because her mama ran off and left us? Should I talk to that counselor at school? Probably just a phase. She is eleven, after all. Maybe hormones ...

No, I was not going to think about that! When the time came for that talk, I would have to get Miss Missouri next door to do the honors. While I went to sit in the park, stuck my fingers in my ears and chanted, "Nah, nah, nah, nah!"

"Daddy?"

My eyes came back into focus and I put the glass down on the table.

"Yes, Katydid?"

"What do you think? Where do people like that live?"

I straightened up and cleared my throat.

"I can't rightly say, Katie. I mean, I never heard of a real …"

I paused and looked away from her and out the window, like something fascinating was happening in the trees across the road for a second.

"That is, I never heard of anyone with wings except people in stories, you know, people like angels and fairies and that sort of thing. And angels live in heaven, I guess, but I don't think they wear cargo pants. Not that I ever saw in the pictures."

I struggled to keep my voice even.

"You did say he was wearing cargo pants, didn't you?"

She nodded her head.

"And a red tee shirt."

"So I guess he's probably not an angel. Not in a red tee shirt. And uh, fairies, well I don't know. They live in Neverland or movies and books, not in town parks. At least, I never heard about any in town parks."

She waited, but I had run out.

"But he was in a town park. I saw him. All the kids saw him."

I wondered if this same conversation was taking place around kitchen tables all over Blakesfield. Maybe the kids all got together and made something up, a joke to play on their parents to liven things up in the hot, dull days of early August, one last hurrah before school started in a couple of weeks.

'Well, sweetie, I don't know what to tell you. I mean, he's not an angel, I don't think. I guess you could ask Brother Wilburn at church on Sunday. Or maybe your Sunday School teacher."

She shook her head.

"No, he's not an angel. Angels all wear long white dresses and have halos over their heads and I'm pretty sure they don't play on swings. You never see pictures of them doing that."

I nodded, but then I wasn't too sure about angels anyway. They looked pretty in those stained glass windows and everything, but something about the whole idea left me cold. Angels sounded like fairy tales to me.

"Do you think he's a fairy or an elf or something like that?" I asked, suddenly realizing that I was curious.

Did I believe in this boy with wings after all?

"Well, I think fairies are all girls and they're real little," she said seriously, screwing up her face. "He's not a girl, and he's not little. He's a regular size for a boy, like the boys in middle school. He doesn't look …"

Her voice trailed off and she frowned.

"He doesn't look … what?" I prodded.

"Well, I guess he might be an elf or something. I mean, his hair is sort of long, not real long but it hangs over his ears. But when the wind was blowing, I could see that it looked like his ears were pointed a little. You know, like Doctor Spock on that old show."

"Mr. Spock," I corrected her. Like I say, we didn't have good TV reception, but I had an old videotape player hooked up to a television and had a collection of old shows. I was a big *Star Trek* fan. Had there been a guy with wings on *Star Trek*? Not Mr. Spock, at any rate.

"Mr. Spock," she repeated. "Anyway, his ears and his eyebrows looked a little like that. You know, pointy."

I rose, picked up the empty glass and took it over to put in the sink. The dishes from dinner were stacked there, waiting for me to wash them. I felt around for the plug and put it in place, turned on the water and shot some liquid detergent onto the pile. Katie got up and went to the cabinets, pulling out a dish towel. I washed, she dried. It was part of our daily routine. We had a dishwasher, but I liked to wash things by hand most of the time. About once a week, I ran a load through the machine, mostly to sanitize things.

I ran a sponge over the dishes and put them carefully into the adjacent sink, running rinse water over them. Katie took them out and put them in the yellow dish rack on the counter and let them drip for a few moments before taking her towel to them. We worked in silence for several minutes, until I had washed and rinsed the last pot.

I scrubbed the sink with the sponge, ran hot water over it and twisted all the water I could out of it before putting it back on the cow-shaped ceramic holder that stood on the window sill above the sink. I looked out the window at Miss Missouri's house next door. She was hanging sheets out to dry on the line where they flapped in the wind that blew all the time out where we lived on the edge of Blakesfield.

Katie kept wiping her towel around the pot, never saying a word and staring at it like the answer to her questions about the boy with wings might be engraved on the aluminum she was rubbing.

I sighed.

"Katie," I turned to her, "are you making this up? 'Cause it's okay if you want to make up stories, but I want you to tell me if you are. Or maybe it was a dream. You know, because of that thunderstorm last night. I know you hate thunderstorms."

She finished wiping the pot, opened the door under the counter and put the pot inside. She closed the door, flicked the towel and then draped it over the dish rack to dry.

"No, Daddy," she finally said, her face scrunched up. "It wasn't a dream and I'm not making it up. He was there. I saw him. And everyone else saw him. You can ask Belinda or Toby. Even that mean old Hank. They'll tell you. Maybe you'll believe them!"

I squatted down so that my face was level with hers, but she turned away and wouldn't look at me. I reached out and drew her into my arms.

"Sweetie, you know I believe you. Most of the time, anyway. But this is weird. A boy with wings? How am I supposed to believe that? In Blakesfield? Not in a book, not on TV, not in a picture. But a barefoot middle school boy playing on a swing. Except he has wings."

She nuzzled my shoulder and said something I couldn't make out. I patted her head and held her close for a minute. Then I gently held her away from me.

"So you saw a boy with wings at the park," I said, keeping doubt and question out of my voice.

"I did," she sniffled. "A real boy. With real wings."

"And you don't know where he came from?"

She shook her head.

"No, he just showed up. Belinda was the first one who saw him. We were just sitting on a bench talking and she pointed at him. He was standing by the edge of the park by the live oaks, watching us. I don't know how long he had been there, and we didn't see which way he came from."

"Is he still there, do you think? Was he there when you came home for supper?"

"No, he left."

I tried to make my voice casual as I asked, "Which way did he go when he left? That might tell us where he's from."

She looked at me and perked up.

"I hadn't thought of that. He flew off down toward the lake."

"Flew off?"

Her head bobbed up and down.

"Yeah, he just got off the swing, turned around and started running toward the slide and then he just sort of rose up in the air and flew off."

"In the direction of the lake?"

"Mmm, hmmm."

Granger's Lake was south of town on the site of an old quarry. It was more of a pond, really, twenty acres at most. The water was amazingly blue against the white rocks that surrounded it. It was a popular hangout for teenagers, but dangerous because the water was deep and there were rocks hidden in the depths. Supposedly an old car was down there, and the boys liked to dive down to try to find it. There were stories about boys diving in and cracking their skulls. I don't know if any of them were true. Certainly it never happened in all the years I had lived in Blakesfield. But I doubt there's a rock quarry in the south that doesn't have stories like that, complete with the old car that had careened over the edge when the brakes failed.

There was nothing much else out there, though, just a few abandoned old sheds from the days when the quarry was being worked. No one lived anywhere near it. I'm not sure who owned the lake, certainly not the town. There were old *Posted* signs hanging around on the barbed wire fence that surrounded it, but those fences had long ago been cut through and hung useless alongside the entrance to the property.

Wonder how much the liability insurance for that place would be? I thought. Maybe that's why no one admits to owning it.

"Well," I finally said, "we'll see what happens. Do you think he'll be back tomorrow?"

She pondered for a moment and shrugged her little shoulders in a way that reminded me of LuNella so much that I felt a stab in my heart. I sure did miss her! I wondered what she would have done if Katie had spun this tale for her?

"Maybe."

A middle school boy with longish hair, pointed ears and eyebrows, silent and winged. Maybe hormones was the answer. Was Katie dreaming up a boyfriend? LuNella would know, but LuNella was gone. Maybe I should ask Miss Missouri. My neighbor was an eighty-five year old widow, but she had raised four girls of her own and had taught grade school forever. She might know what this was all about.

Chapter 3

August days are long in our part of Texas. When Katie went to her room to read, I got out my bicycle and decided to ride around town and clear my head.

Blakesfield is in Central Texas, in Windham County. There's not much out our way and the town motto is "West of the Beyond." As I said, there is no industry, the farms and ranches have pretty much blown away and my family's once-prosperous Peck Pecan Orchards had folded during the 1998 drought. My brother Richard was trying to get it going again, but it was early days, early days. I wasn't on speaking terms with Richard or anyone else in the family. So I had no idea how that was going.

During the fall and winter, hunters came in from all over the place, especially from the big cities, to bag deer or wild turkeys. That provided enough additional revenue to maintain a couple of gas stations, a feed store, a taxidermist and a couple of small eateries. Richard, or so I hear by the grapevine, had been talking about turning part of the old orchards into an exotic animal hunting ranch. The thought of portly insurance executives from Dallas being driven around our old property to shoot gazelles while sipping martinis from silver flasks made me sick. But my own drinking is one reason I had no say in what happens out there these days.

What was left of a place called Arena was ten miles away. It used to be a stopping place between Blakesfield and the county seat in Davis, back in the days when the roads were mostly winding paths of packed earth and stone. When good paved roads came, however, they put in straight roads between the main markets. The big trucks took the bypass around Arena and it was soon mostly a ghost town.

When I was a kid, we would ride our bikes and later as a teenager, drive our cars out there and sneak into one of the three abandoned houses that were still standing. It was a great place to drink, scare your date with a spooky story and make out. There was an old one room schoolhouse that hadn't been used since the 1930s and a Methodist Church that was still used by a handful of local farming families. In its heyday, Arena had boasted a Baptist Church, a Holiness Tabernacle and a Church of Christ building, but those had all been torn down about ten years ago.

Lately we started hearing rumors that some developer from Austin had been talking about putting up something in Arena to lure people who wanted to experience rural living. I wished him luck. They didn't say we were west of the beyond for no reason. Even if Richard went through with his African game park idea, that would cater to people who had no interest in relocating out here. They would want to drive in, shoot a trophy animal and head back home to brag in the comfort of their Preston Hollow estates close to their downtown Big D offices.

Maybe that developer was looking things over because of another rumor. There was a lot of talk about some power companies coming through and putting in one of those electricity-generating windmill farms. They were springing up all over parts of Texas. I was up in the Panhandle last year and there were places where those giant white fans stretched as far as the eye could see. It might work in Blakesfield.

"Lord knows," Wayne said to me the other day when we were on our way to a meeting in Cherokee Creek, "if there's one thing we have around here, it's blowhards."

Katie, Billy Bob and I lived in a big house on the edge of town. When LuNella and I got married, my folks thought she was going to get me to settle down. They built a nice brick house for us on twenty acres not far from the Peck Pecan Orchards. I turned my bike toward town with my back to what remained of the orchards.

I hated the orchards. When they were going great guns, they made my mama's family the richest folks in Windham County. She raised me and Richard to think we were better than everyone else, when all we were was richer. She meant well, I supposed. I liked to think so. It's hard to think bad about your own mama.

My father made us work in the orchards when we were teenagers, and I resented that. It's not so hard to think bad things about your daddy. We didn't need to earn money, I would remind him. We had tons of it. Let people who needed jobs work in the

Texas weather. I was made for better things. I was going off to college and become a professor or something. I was not going to run a nut farm. That was my derogatory term for it – the nut farm. Richard always called it The Orchards. With capital letters.

Little jerk!

Despite my constant insistence that I would never work for the orchards, my father hoped I would come to work there once I found out that the job market for college professors was pretty thin on the ground. I did discover that, about the same time I discovered that being the smartest kid in Blakesfield and Cherokee Creek doesn't mean a whole lot when you swim into a bigger pond.

I went to Rice University, got my degree in philosophy, couldn't find a job, and like so many of my ilk, went back for another degree. Still couldn't find a job. Humiliated by my failure and nagged by LuNella to do something, I broke down and gave the orchards a try. They put me in an office with a computer and a secretary, but I was not made for business. It bored me to tears and I never managed to find my wings.

Wings.

There was little traffic on FM 376 and in the late summer heat, water mirages receded in front of me as I pedaled along. I passed the Blakesfield School Campus, a grandiose name for three small buildings that housed an elementary school, a middle school and administrative offices. The fenced and locked playground lay behind them. Dust devils spun across the yard, picking up and dropping scraps of paper.

Blakesfield was not big enough for a high school. Students that age were bused fifteen miles to a consolidated school at Cherokee Creek. Cherokee Creek was not incorporated but the school was a six-man football powerhouse. Six-man football, as you can probably figure out if you don't already know, is a variation of regular American – the only *real* football, as any Texan will tell you – with teams consisting of six men instead of eleven and played on an eighty yard field. There's also eight-man football, but we weren't even big enough for that.

Since football, not cleanliness, was next to godliness in the Great State of Texas, if a school was too small for regular football, they did everything in their power to field at least a six-man team. At last count, there were well over two hundred such teams in the state. And that is not counting schools that fielded a regular team and so-called "outlaw teams" of six men so that more of their students could play. I never played football of either variety, but my best friend during my school years, Hank Ingram, was the star quarterback at Cherokee Creek.

Just past the schools, I turned right and rode along Church Street. First there was Saint Maura Catholic Mission, where an unfriendly old Irish missionary celebrated Latin Mass every other Sunday. It shared a parking lot, though nothing else, with the Holiness Tabernacle Church of God in Christ. A vacant lot was between the Tabernacle and Good Shepherd Methodist Church. On the other side of the street were the Bible Baptist Church, Evangel Temple and the Church of Christ.

Church Street was a dead end, a source of much amusement to the handful of locals who were not religious. I turned my bike around in the Church of Christ parking lot and headed back to the farm-to-market road and then onto the main drag.

"It's a drag all right!" generations of Blakesfield high school students said, as they drove up and down, up and down the short stretch of the business district. Each generation thought it had invented the joke and that it was terribly witty.

I rode past the Café Texan and Tiny's Dinette, the Fina and Valero stations, past empty storefronts topped by a faded Mercantile sign, bounced across rusted railroad tracks and glanced at the collapsing corrugated tin shed where they used to store supplies for the train. The last train rolled through when I was in high school.

Just beyond the last storefront was a town limit sign with the population: 1129.

I wheeled my bike around and headed back toward home. Time to talk to Wayne.

Wayne was my sponsor. He worked as a cook at Tiny's Dinette, had enormous heavily tattooed arms, had been divorced two or three times – it was never clear to me how many of his women he actually married – and had been sober thirteen years. As far as I could tell, he lived on and by the slogans that contain a lot of the program's experience and wisdom.

Easy Does It.

One Day at a Time.

First Things First.

Wayne was my personal Yoda, Jiminy Cricket and Dalai Lama. I drove him crazy.

He told me to call him whenever I needed help, and the Central Texas air had not yet pushed Katie's story out of my head. I wanted a good shot of Wayne's common sense to get me back on an even keel.

When I pulled the bike up to Tiny's Dinette, there were no cars in the packed white rock parking lot. I leaned the bike up against the end of the building and went in.

An old man was sitting in a booth against the far wall, poking his fork into what I guessed was the special of the day. I thought the world of Wayne, but Tiny's specials were another matter. They usually featured melted Velveeta, ground beef, chopped peppers and onions, all surrounded by an orange rim of grease. The only AA slogan that they called to mind was a hopeful *This Too Shall Pass*.

Except during the fall and winter hunting seasons, Tiny's didn't run to waitresses. You went to the counter, rang a bell and gave your order. When it was done, they called your name and you went and picked it up.

Tiny's didn't bother to give you numbers. They knew everyone who ate there by name, and if they didn't know you, they would just yell out, "Hey, the guy who wanted the Taquerito Deluxe, it's ready if you're still interested."

I went up to the counter and tapped on the bell.

Wayne poked his head up and looked through the open space between the kitchen and the dining area.

"What'cha need, Corny?" he asked. "Something for dinner for you and the kids? Our special's real good tonight. The freezer broke and I have to use up some steaks. Real good price, and nobody's died yet, so far as I know."

The old man in the booth snorted loudly.

Not sure how much I wanted to trust steaks from a broken freezer, I shook my head.

"No, we already ate. I just want some food for thought if you've got a minute."

"Come on back," he said, going over and holding the kitchen door open. "Tiny's gone over to the Texan to get his own dinner and he usually stays and chews the chicken fat with Elliot when he's done."

Elliot was the owner of Tiny's rival establishment, the Café Texan. The two men were great friends and liked to commiserate over the sad economic conditions in Blakesfield and ponder how to get the town council to permit the sale of beer and wine to improve their restaurant business. Seeing as how the town manager and town treasurer were joint owners of the liquor store and a bar and grill in Cherokee Creek, it seemed unlikely that they would be open to allowing competition to move into Blakesfield. But political reality never prevented Texans from planning and plotting. For that matter, reality of any kind seldom made much of an impression on Texans.

I should know. I am a sixth-generation Texan. On my mother's side, anyway, the Peck side.

I found an empty stool in the corner and perched on it while Tiny went back to chopping and bagging lettuce.

"People in this town eat salad?" I asked.

"Not much, but this iceberg stuff is cheap and you can fill up half a meatloaf plate with it, toss on a paper-thin slice of tomato and a dab of French dressing and call it a side salad. Don't fool nobody but it don't hurt and it makes the plate look full."

He sealed a couple of bags and tossed them into an old avocado-colored Frigidaire.

"Did you come here to talk about salad?"

"No," I said, shifting on the uncomfortable wooden seat of the stool. "It's Katie."

Wayne stole a glance at the front to make sure no one was waiting and turned his attention back to me.

"Something wrong with Katie?"

I shrugged.

"I don't know. She told me this crazy story about a kid with wings today. I don't know what to make of it. She doesn't make stuff up, you know. Not usually. And she seemed really serious."

Wayne looked at me.

"Well, why is it bothering you, then? Maybe it's true."

I looked at him.

True?

In the program we are supposed to have a Higher Power on whom (or on which) we rely to help stay sober. It can be anyone or anything you want, however you want to understand it. Sometimes you hear someone say, "the God of my understanding" or "my higher power who I choose to call God" or something of that nature. The grammatical purist in me cringes: "***whom*** I choose to call God," I have been tempted to shout. My favorite version is my friend Steve's, who always talks about "the God of my misunderstanding."

When I first started coming to meetings, I heard someone talking about how he stayed sober with the help of his HP. I thought he meant his Hewlett Packard and imagined him talking to his computer's printer. Didn't sound sober to me!

Most people, I guess, just kept believing in the God they always believed in, although a lot of them changed their mind about what God was really like. My impression was that the God/Higher Power that people in the program talked about was a sight friendlier than the God a lot of them grew up with.

Some people just took the group as their Higher Power. They didn't think it was divine or anything, but they counted on the group for support and wisdom and help. The program said Higher Power; technically it didn't say Highest Power.

Other people chose what I would call downright weird Higher Powers. One woman I knew swore that her first Higher Power was her gerbil and that kept her sober for years before she came around to a more traditional approach.

And then there's the guy who picked one of the old pecan trees on the ridge outside of town. It was big and solid and had stood out in the Central Texas heat and winds since at least the time Sam Houston was president of the Republic of Texas. There was no way to know how long it had stood there before Santa Ana went down in defeat at San Jacinto one April afternoon in 1836.

Eddie G counted on that tree for a long time, and then disaster struck.

Just a week after I quit drinking and asked Wayne to be my sponsor, he called me up and said, "You're going to go with me on a service call."

That scared me. I thought he meant we were going to go talk to some drunk in a hospital somewhere and try to get him sober. I wasn't ready for anything like that. I wasn't sure I was sober myself yet. But when I climbed into the back of Wayne's battered old Jeep, Eddie G was sitting up front, looking like a man who had had a shock.

"What's the deal?" I asked.

Bouncing up and down as we turned down one dirt road after another, Wayne explained that Eddie G's tree had been hit by lightning and we were looking for another one. We spent an hour and a half, driving along ridges, looking at lots of trees that looked like they had been there since the Flood at least, assuming Noah's deluge had bothered to wash over the dry lands of Central Texas. But Eddie kept shaking his head.

"I'll know it when I see it," he kept saying.

And finally he found the one he wanted. Personally I thought it looked pretty beat up, and I suggested maybe he wanted one that looked more robust, one that would last longer. I knew from painful family experience that as hardy as Texas pecan trees are, they are not invulnerable.

"No," Eddie said, circling the tree and viewing it from every angle. "I'm a pretty beat up old dude myself, and I think this old tree is just what I need to see me through."

He walked over and patted the tree.

"Will you be my sponsor?" he asked quietly.

I grinned at Wayne, but Wayne's face was serious. If Eddie G wanted this tree to be his sponsor, who were we to question it?

I guess he got the answer he wanted, because Eddie patted the tree a couple more times and said, "Fine. I'll be in touch."

We all climbed back in the Jeep and headed into town, Eddie chatting amiably about how much he was going to miss that old tree and how grateful he was that we had gone with him to find his new one.

Chapter 4

I'm not too sure about Wayne's Higher Power. He clearly has one, but he doesn't say much about it. Or him. Or her, for that matter. I'm pretty sure it's not Jesus or God in the conventional sense. Wayne never says, "My Higher Power, who I choose to call God …". If he says anything, he just says, "My Higher Power."

I know he goes to Mass at St. Maura's. I asked him once if he liked the Latin, but he said he didn't understand a word of it.

"No, I like to just go and sit and think. Since it's in another language, I don't have to pay any attention to it at all. Works just fine for me. Kind of background noise. It doesn't distract me like most of the other places people go of a Sunday morning."

I had been brought up Catholic. Maybe I would still be going to Mass if I were like Wayne and didn't understand what they were saying. It was understanding, or thinking I understood, that caused the problems.

At any rate, maybe WhatEver or WhomEver Wayne believed in was the kind of What or Who that made believing in boys with wings an easy thing. Maybe like that character in *Alice in Wonderland* who believed six impossible things every day before breakfast.

"What do you mean, it might be true? There's no such thing as boys with wings," I said, staring at him.

"Well," he drawled, "I admit I ain't never seen one. Leastways, not since I been sober. But there's lots of things I ain't seen, but that don't mean those things ain't real."

I shook my head. So much for Wayne's common sense getting me back to normal.

"Wayne, seriously, man! Katie said this kid showed up at the park and he had wings. Not I know that's not true, because –"

"Because why?" he interrupted. "Because you never saw a boy with wings. That's your reason, isn't it?"

"Heck, yeah, that's my reason! That's the only reason there needs to be, because what doesn't exist anywhere, doesn't exist at

Peck's Park in Blakesfield, Texas. It's a basic philosophical principle."

I wasn't sure about that, but I figured Wayne wouldn't challenge me on philosophy. He knows I have university degrees, although that doesn't impress him too much.

"Okay, first things first. Are you going to drink over this?"

"Hell, no! I mean, no. Why would I?"

"I don't know. You just seem pretty bent out of shape over it. How do I know what makes you drink?"

I sighed.

"Everything used to make me drink. But not now. I quit. You know that. I quit."

He waited a moment and then asked, "Still got that beer in the fridge?"

"It's ale, and yes," I admitted. "But it's there for a reason. You know that."

"So you say," he muttered. "Anyway, you're not gonna drink?"

"No, I'm not gonna drink."

"All right. That's the main thing. Did Katie say anyone else saw it?"

"Yeah, she said all the kids saw him. Saw it. Whatever."

"Did you ask any of the other kids? Or any of their parents?"

I was getting angry.

"There's no goddamn reason to go asking any kids or anyone else. You and I both know it didn't happen."

"You're wrong," Wayne said, pulling a dripping head of lettuce out of the big sink where it had been soaking in cold water. "You say you know it didn't happen. I don't know it didn't happen. All I know is Katie said it happened, Katie said she was telling the truth, Katie said there were witnesses who would back her up, and according to you, Katie doesn't make up stuff."

He chopped the head of lettuce in half with a single blow, turned the halves on their sides and quickly finished hacking them into bite-size pieces. I watched in silence. He worked his way through two more heads, bagged the results and tossed the bags into the refrigerator.

"Okay," I said as he turned back toward the sink, "what are you saying?"

"There is something somewhere in the Big Book in that section on spiritual experience. Something about contempt prior to investigation. You know, when you have an idea that you are so firmly convinced about that it is a barrier against all information and proof against all arguments. But if it is wrong, all it does it keep you ignorant. Sounds to me like you are guilty of contempt prior to investigation."

I jumped off the stool, put it back in the corner and walked out.

"You're just *ferhoodled*!" he called after me, using one of his pet words he picked up from some Amish girlfriend back in the day.

Fat lot of help that had been! Quoting the Big Book at me, like some blankety-blank, puke-faced Baptist Sunday School teacher. This didn't have anything to do with the Big Book, it didn't have anything to do with my alcoholism. This had to do with some wild tale my daughter was telling and I wanted to know what it meant.

And one thing I was damned well sure it did not mean: That there were boys with wings flying around Windham County.

I made up a syllogism:

1) There are no winged boys any place.
2) Blakesfield is a place.
3) Therefore, there are no winged boys in Blakesfield.

I was satisfied until I realized that as sound as that sounded, it was a classic case of *petitio principii*, what is commonly known as circular reasoning. My first statement is an assumption that is not proved by my syllogism.

But, dammit, there ***were*** no winged boys any place. No way, no how, never had been, never would be. You didn't need a formal syllogism to know that any more than you needed one to know water was wet.

I ground my teeth all the way home.

I thought about stopping at Miss Missouri's place to talk to her about all this, but her lights were out when I rode by. She turned in early and watched television until it put her to sleep. Then she complained that it didn't work and she was up later and later. She talked to her doctor about her sleeping problems and the doctor asked if she watched Fox News.

"Of course, I watch it all day long." Miss Missouri told her.

"Stop watching Fox News," the doctor said.

Miss Missouri laughed but kept watching it. And kept having trouble sleeping.

I would talk to her first thing in the morning, I told myself. Well, first thing after I asked Katie if she still wanted to claim her story was true.

As I put the bike back in the garage, I found myself wondering if maybe this did have something to do with my alcoholism. I quit drinking five months ago, but Wayne said I wasn't making any progress on the steps.

The first step, admitting I was powerless over alcohol and that my life had become unmanageable was easy. Or so I told him. He thought me keeping that bottle of ale in the refrigerator was a sign I believed I did have power over alcohol. And that one reason I was having trouble with the next step, coming to believe that a power greater than myself cold restore me to sanity, was that I still thought I could do it on my own. That I thought there wasn't any power greater than myself.

I kicked the bike and walked out of the garage and around the end of the house into the back yard. A big swing set stood in the middle of the yard, a Christmas gift for Katie when she was six. I lowered my butt onto one of the swings and pushed back and forth, staring out at the darkening sky where the stars were starting to appear.

"The stars at night
Are big and bright,"
I warbled softly off key,
"Deep in the heart of Texas.
The prairie sky

Is high and wide,
Deep in the heart of Texas."

I heard the screen door open behind me.

"Daddy?" Katie called. "Is that you?"

I got up and walked toward the house. I tried to put a smile in my voice.

"It's me, sweetie, deep in the heart of Texas."

I put my arm around her and we went into the house.

Chapter 5

The next morning after I got Katie and Billy Bob fed, I got him into his stroller and sent Katie out to walk him around in the fresh air while it was still cool. Well, cool by Central Texas standards. By eight in the morning it was already getting up into the low 80s.

There were no sidewalks in our neighborhood. Shoot, there weren't a lot of neighbors in our neighborhood. Our house was on a twenty acre plot and Miss Missouri's sat on ten acres, and then there was a stretch of weedy scrub brush for half a mile before you came on another house. Miss Missouri and her husband Frank had been the only people on that road for many years. When my parents built the house for me and LuNella, my father looked into buying a hundred acres or so and starting a development of some sort. This was before the collapse of the orchard business. He was bad about listening to the advice of the county extension guys as far as taking care of the pecan trees was concerned – hence the collapse of the orchards – but when it came to investing in land, he admitted he didn't know everything and consulted local realtors and bankers. They told him there was never going to be much market for housing out there, not unless some unforeseen industrial development came to town. At the time, there was none on the horizon. And he gave up on that idea.

He had gone so far as to have someone make a fancy sign that read "Southwood Drive." I helped him put it up on the corner where our dirt road intersected with the farm-to-market road. Five years later, that name started showing up on maps. So I guessed it was official now, even though our mail was still addressed to a rural route box number.

Katie headed off past Miss Missouri's house, keeping well to the side of the road and in what little shade there was. Billy Bob loved to be pushed in the stroller and I could hear him laughing and cooing until they passed Miss Missouri's. She was out in her yard, sweeping leaves and dirt off her driveway, and she called out to them and waved. Katie waved back but kept walking.

Miss Missouri looked back at our house, saw me in the yard and lifted her hand in greeting. I decided that was as good a time as any to consult her about Katie's story.

Miss Missouri was a tiny old woman with eyes that were still a clear blue behind her glasses and white hair that she had fixed every Friday at Danelle's Hair Fantasia out on Davis Highway.

Danelle was Miss Missouri's cousin in one of those connections that are ubiquitous in small towns. For all I knew, Danelle was one of my distant cousins, too. She ran a small beauty parlor out of a room her husband built onto the side of their house, and she did a booming business giving the ladies of Miss Missouri's generation the same hair style and perms they had been wearing since Jack Kennedy was president.

LuNella always refused to go to Danelle, saying she didn't want to look like her great-aunts, thank you very much. She went to a stylist over in Davis, who talked to her about people we didn't know and charged her twice as much as Danelle would have. Plus Danelle's gossip would have been more interesting, being about people we knew and all. And LuNella was so beautiful, she would have looked great even in one of Danelle's cuts.

"Morning, Miss Missouri," I said, sauntering across our lawns.

"Mornin' Corny," she said, still sweeping the drive. "I see Katie's out with Billy Bob."

"Yes'm. I like her to take him for some air before it gets too hot."

She nodded and swept at a particularly stubborn pile of dirt.

"I swan, you'd think this place would of blowed away by now," she remarked.

"Hmmm," I said, noncommittally.

If I had heard that once, I had heard it a thousand times. The winds blew all the time in Blakesfield. I guess that was one reason it would be a good place for one of those windmill farms.

"Miss Missouri, can I ask you something?"

She stopped sweeping and looked at me through smudged glasses.

"Of course, Corny. Is there a problem?"

I put my hands in my hip pockets and rocked back and forth on my feet.

"I don't rightly know. Katie came home with this crazy story yesterday. She doesn't usually make things up or lie. And she insists that it's true. But I know it can't be and don't know what to make of it."

"Do you want a cup of coffee?" she asked, heading toward her house. "I'm going to get myself one. Come inside and talk."

I followed her in through the glassed-in porch that stretched half the length of her house.

She told me once that when she and Frank built the house, it had a regular open porch. But the constant wind just blew stuff up on the porch to be tracked into the house, and so they had the porch glassed in. The wind still blew stuff through the door onto the porch, but less of it made its way into her home.

"I'm sorry this place is such a mess," she said, walking through an immaculate and uncluttered living room and into a kitchen that looked like it was never used. "My sister Wanda Mae keeps her place so clean, but I never can keep up with it all."

Wanda Mae, unlike Miss Missouri, had never worked outside her home. She was a sweet and funny old lady, but her house was her world. I don't think she ever let a dust particle settle on the floor if she saw it still in the air. Her husband had kept a few cattle and drove a tractor trailer. She said she had to keep cleaning because he kept bringing mess into the house every time he came back from taking care of the cows or when he got back from a month on the road. She had been a widow for ten years, but she still kept the house polished.

LuNella had been a good housekeeper, but she thought there was more to life than sweeping and mopping. She bought every labor-saving device she heard of and still claimed she needed someone to come in twice a week to help out. When she left us, I sort of let it all go to blazes.

I'm not the house-proud type. I remember years ago reading that some Englishman had said that after two years the dust doesn't get any worse. That may not be true in our part of Texas, but I was willing to see.

Fortunately Ada, the woman who came in to help LuNella, kept coming twice a week, did the kids' laundry – "You're big enough to do your own laundry, Mr. Corny," she told me firmly – and kept the place respectable. So I never found out if the two-year rule worked as well in Blakesfield as it did in London. My house's state was no comparison to Miss Missouri's, much less Miss Wanda Mae's, but Katie could have friends over without being embarrassed by the way she lived.

"No coffee, thanks," I called. "I just had breakfast."

I sat down on a red-and-gold brocade sofa and waited for her to return.

"Come in here and sit at the table," she called, leading me through the kitchen to a small dining room. She put her mug down and lowered herself into one of the wooden chairs. The mug said, "Miss Missouri, We'll miss U!" The words were faded and rubbed from many years of use and cleaning. It had been a gift from the last class of fifth graders she taught. That was so many years ago that most of those students had kids of their own in school now.

I explained about Katie and the boy with wings.

"What do I do?" I asked. "Did your girls ever tell tall tales like that? Should I be worried? Do you think it's because she's getting to be … well, she's eleven and maybe she's starting to notice boys?"

Miss Missouri sipped her coffee and looked at me over the mug. When she put it down, she had a huge grin on her face.

"Corny Adams, you are an idiot," she said affectionately.

"I know," I said. "But that's a whole 'nother story. And maybe that's why I'm asking you about this. I don't know what to do."

"So Katie saw the winged boy, too," she said musingly.

I turned a startled face towards her.

"What do you mean, saw the winged boy, too? Don't tell me you saw it. Him. It."

She shook her head.

"No, I haven't seen him. Not yet, but I may go down to Peck's Park later to see if he shows up again. Wanda Mae called me last night to tell me her grandson Chase came running to her house crying because his daddy whipped him for lying when he told that story. Wanda Mae hugged him and told him it was all right, and then she called her boy Jerry up and chewed him out for hitting that boy. 'I told him, if I had whupped you for every story you told when you was Chase's age, you might not have growed up at all.' That's what she told me she said, anyway. I'm not so sure Jerry did grow up, but I didn't tell Wanda Mae that. You know how mamas are about their kids. They can gripe till the cows come home but nobody else better say boo."

She laughed gently.

"But don't you think maybe the kids got together and made this all up?" I asked.

Chase was about Katie's age and a bit of a pill, as we say around here. It wouldn't surprise me to know he was the one who made up this story and then got Katie and some of the other kids to go along with it. They must be bored enough by now with the summer heat draining their energy and their parents more than ready to send them back to school for six hours a day.

Miss Missouri shook her head.

"I think maybe it's real."

I clenched my teeth and frowned.

"No, not *real* real," she went on, "just something they saw and maybe don't understand. Maybe he had some sort of wings on his shirt or something."

I nodded my head.

"I thought of that," I admitted, "but it doesn't sound like something a boy that age would do. Not a boy out here in the middle of the Texas hill country."

"Oh, you're thinking of those wings the girls wear at Halloween and stuff," she said. "No, I don't see that happening either. But you know, when Wanda Mae and I were in Austin a few months back shopping for bras, I saw a lot of tee shirts that had wings printed on the back of them. They seemed to be real popular with the kids. Maybe he just had on one of those tee shirts and the kids let their imaginations run away with them."

It made some sense. I've heard it said that we Texans don't lie. We just tell more truth than there is. And one highly regarded history prof that I had at Rice University used to say that you should never let the truth get in the way of a good story.

"You think that's all it is?" I said, hope in my voice.

I liked this solution. It still meant I needed to sit down with Katie and explain to her the line between what happened and what didn't happen but sounds more interesting. Maybe it wasn't boys so much as just her growing up and needing to learn to distinguish between the fairy tales she loved and the real world she was going to have to live in. We all have to learn that, right?

"Maybe," said Miss Missouri. "But I'll tell you something, Corny. I kind of wish it were true. Wouldn't that be nice? What do you suppose it would mean? Think he'd be an angel?"

"Well, Katie said he wasn't an angel or a fairy or anything like that. She said he looked just like any other kid that age, but he had wings."

Miss Missouri laughed again.

"It's the ultimate fantasy for kids, you know, being able to fly. Didn't you run around with a towel around your neck and hanging down your back, pretending to be Superman or someone, arms out in front of you and swooshing?"

Of course, I had. What red-blooded kid hadn't done that? And when I saw a stage production of *Peter Pan* when I was seven, I was convinced that happy thoughts and some pixie dust would have done the trick for me.

On stage, they had used glitter to represent Tinkerbell's dust. I found some silver glitter in my mother's craft drawer and I ran around the house, tossing handfuls into the air and running through it, thinking the happiest thoughts I could.

This did not result in my flying, but there was lots of crying when my mother caught me and gave me a whipping after her maid Ella told on me. It was an early lesson in the difference between stories and reality. I squirmed a little in Miss Missouri's hard wooden chair as I remembered it.

She looked at her mug and put it down.

"Anyway, Corny, don't worry about it. It won't hurt Katie to be a child a little longer and believe in boys who fly. Trust me, she will be growing up way too fast, way too soon. And it won't be boys with wings you have to worry about then."

Well, if that was meant to make me feel better somehow, it failed miserably.

Chapter 6

Later in the morning, I called Wayne to check in. I figured he was pissed off because I just walked out on him the night before, but he got over stuff fast. Which was good for me, because I realized I had acted like an ass. The Tenth Step said when I was wrong, I needed to admit it promptly. But, I told myself in my best-practiced rationalizing manner, I wasn't at the Tenth Step yet.

"The steps are in order for a reason," people said. "Each step builds on the ones that go before it."

I knew in my heart of hearts that this did not absolve me from the need to apologize for being a jerk. But what the hey.

Wayne's phone immediately went to voice mail. I left a message that I needed to talk to him, but it wasn't urgent.

Katie was having lunch over at Belinda's house, and I took Billy Bob to Miss Missouri and asked if she could look after him for the afternoon. She lit up and reached for him. I handed him over, kissed him on the head and thanked her.

Then I went for a bike ride. I do a lot of that.

I don't know if I mentioned that when LuNella left me, I took the kids next door to Miss Missouri's and went out and got roaring drunk. That was how I dealt with problems, getting drunk. That was also how I dealt with celebrations, too, getting drunk. It was how I dealt with Sundays, Mondays, Tuesdays, Wednesdays … well, you get the idea.

Most of the time the worst thing I had to deal with was a hangover, but that night on my way back from the bar in Cherokee Creek, flashing lights in my rear view mirror signaled something really bad.

I wasn't worried at first, though. Everybody and his brother, including all the deputy sheriffs, knew that I had gotten a free pass most times when I was pulled over and given a warning. That time my luck had run out. The fresh-faced new deputy wasn't from around there and my name and the Peck Orchards money meant nothing to him

I became a guest of Windham County for three days, paid a fine of $4,000 and had my license suspended for six months. That may sound a bit much for a first offense, but then, it wasn't my first offense. I got a DUI when I was away in college in Houston, where my name and the Peck Orchards money didn't make any impression either. Although that had been years ago, in Texas it stayed on my record.

When I got back home after three days in jail, when I saw the look on Katie's face, I swore I would not do that ever again. Swore to myself, not just to her. And I hadn't had a drink in the five months since.

That same day I fished in my pocket for the card they gave me in jail and called the number for Alcoholics Anonymous. A recorded voice told me there was a meeting in Cherokee Creek that night. Which was fine except I couldn't drive.

Then I remembered Wayne.

Once when I was staggering around in Tiny's after a night of too much booze and not enough sense, Wayne had looked at me over the counter and said calmly, "You know, you don't ever have to feel this bad again. When you want help, you know where to find me."

I didn't have the bike yet, and I had to walk down to Tiny's that afternoon and ask for a ride to the meeting. I had been riding over there to the Presbyterian Church with Wayne twice a week ever since. After the first two meetings, I asked him to be my sponsor. We were stuck in his Jeep together for almost an hour twice a week, and I figured I might as well use the time.

The meetings were okay but I didn't enjoy them all that much. When Wayne asked me what I thought about a meeting one night on our way back to Blakesfield, I said that I didn't learn much, that the conversation had been rather desultory, never finding a focus.

"Desultory," he said with a snort. "You don't need to use a six-bit word when a penny one will do the job."

I blushed in the dark, because I knew it was pompous when I said it.

I don't know if you know much about AA. Everybody's heard about it, but if you're like I was, you don't know anything about how it works or just about everything you know is wrong. That doesn't matter for this story, and I'm not going to waste time telling you all about it. If you need to know, you can find out. Look in the telephone directory, go online and do a search, ask a cop or a librarian. Someone will know where to point you.

I'm not going to tell you everything, but since I was just five months sober, AA was a big part of my life right then. I had done Step One. More or less. I thought more, Wayne thought less. I knew I was an alcoholic. I knew I couldn't take a single drink.

Let me explain that. I could ***not*** take a single drink. That is, I could choose not to pick up the first drink. What I was unable to do was take a ***single*** drink. I was the incarnation of the old saying, "First the man takes a drink; then the drink takes a drink; then the drink takes the man." As they say in the program – trust me, they have a million of these – One drink was too many and a hundred was never enough.

So I knew I was powerless over alcohol once it was in my system. This was my understanding of what it meant for me to be an alcoholic. Just because someone drank heavily didn't mean that person was an alcoholic. Even if someone abused alcohol, they might not be an alcoholic. As long as they could drink one and walk away when they wanted to, they could do something this alcoholic could not. More power to them. But it didn't work that way for me.

The rest of Step One was admitting my life had become unmanageable. Okay, I spent three days in jail, paid a small fortune in fines, lost my wife to a typewriter repairman – Heck, what did he repair? Did anyone still use typewriters? – and now I was a single dad with a Lexus in the garage and no driver's license, trying to raise two kids on his own. My life was unmanageable.

Maybe that was why I was thrown by Katie's story. She had always been so easy to deal with. I didn't have to manage her at all. She managed herself. I guessed I should give LuNella credit for raising her right, but I wasn't quite there yet. Given time, maybe I'd make it. But not yet.

Anyway, I thought the one part of my life that was under control was Katie. And now she came in with this cock-and-bull story. It felt like everything was going to start slipping through my fingers again, just when I thought I was getting a grip.

I hopped on the bike and headed down to Tiny's. Maybe I could catch Wayne before the lunch hour rush. Rush was hardly the word. There weren't enough people in Blakesfield to create a rush. A slight uptick maybe.

My own phone started ringing just as I was pulling into the parking lot. It was Wayne's ring, "Friends in Low Places." I got off the bike and pulled the phone out of my pocket.

"Wayne, hey. You busy?"

He muttered that he was trying to cope with a delivery and get ready for lunch at the same time. Could it wait?

"I guess," I said, disappointed.

I counted on Wayne a lot. He hinted from time to time that I counted on him too much.

"Quick question," he said. "Are you going to drink?"

"No, it's just this thing with Katie. I still don't know what to do."

I could hear a long exhale on the phone.

"Do you have to do anything? Just easy does it, okay? Ride that bike out into the country ten miles, turn around and ride back. It will do you good to get tired and we can talk about it later. Right now I can't. I got to go back to work."

"Okay," I said, but he interrupted before I could turn off the phone.

"Did you do your readings this morning?"

Wayne wants me to read three pages in the Big Book and spend some time in prayer and meditation each morning. AA is the original spiritual-but-not-religious program.

"No," I admitted, wondering if I could have fooled him with a lie.

"That's the problem, son. It only works if you work it. Gotta go."

And he clicked off.

It only works if you work it. Another one of those damned bumper sticker slogans.

I climbed back on my bike and circled the lot, wondering whether I should go back home and read the stuff I had skipped or take his other advice and take a long ride out into the country. My body made the decision and I headed out of town.

Chapter 7

My body was leaving town, but my mind was still tussling with AA.

I was supposed to be working on Step Two. That's the one about believing a power greater than myself could restore me to sanity.

I'm an agnostic. I'm probably really an atheist, if I'm going to be rigorously honest about it. (*Rigorous honesty* is another catchword in the program. So is *program.*) But I've always hedged my bets. Always been afraid to commit.

My mama says I drove her crazy when I was a kid and she would give me a dollar to buy something in the dime store. Of course, by then you couldn't buy much of anything for a dime, but around here folks still called it a dime store. The old folks said five-and-dime. I guess that meant there had been a time when you could get something for a nickel.

Anyway, I would wander up and down the aisles, staring at toys and looking at prices and picking up one thing and putting it back, and then another and then another. It would take me forever to find something that I wanted bad enough to part with my dollar. I always thought there might be a better choice in the next aisle. Or the next one. I usually didn't decide until she threatened to take the dollar back and make me go home with nothing. Then I grabbed something and went home to wonder what might have been.

I was still that kid clinging to his dollar when it came to the idea of a Higher Power. I'm pretty sure I'm not God, but I'm not at all sure what I want that Higher Power to be. Like I said, some people pick a tree or a pet or the AA group. They always tell you it's entirely up to you, but it still sounds to me like they expect you to pick Jesus eventually. Even the Big Book hints at this, the way I read it. I like Jesus and all, but I can't deal with all the trimmings.

"Lord, protect me from your followers."

That's my personal bumper sticker slogan, although I would never mess up my Lexus by putting a bumper sticker on it.

So I'm still looking for a Higher Power.

As usual, Wayne's advice was good. I worked up a good sweat on that long ride in the early afternoon sun, and by the time I got back to the house and took a shower, I felt better. Maybe he and Miss Missouri were right. Maybe I could just wait this out. The kids would get tired of the story pretty soon. If I got all agitated, that would probably make them keep at it longer.

Be cool, that was the ticket. Cool and serene. Accept the things I cannot change, and all that crap. I toweled off, put on a pair of clean jeans and tee shirt and went to look in the freezer to see what to make for dinner.

I got some chicken tenders out to thaw. I didn't eat all that much red meat any more, which is decidedly a non-Texan attitude, but that's the way it is. Katie, like most kids, could live on chicken nuggets in one form or another, and I had found an easy recipe to make them in the oven. I would heat up some barbecue sauce for a dip. She would eat hers with ketchup, but I like a little more bite in my bites.

That decided, I went next door to get Billy Bob. Miss Missouri had just put him down for a nap and said she didn't want to wake him up.

"You've got enough on your mind, and he's a sweetie. No trouble at all. I'll bring him over when he wakes up. He'll want something to eat by then, I imagine, and I don't have anything in the house fit for a growing boy."

I thanked her and headed back home.

Katie was nowhere in sight, down at Peck's Park, I figured. I considered walking down there and then thought better of it. I didn't want her thinking I was checking up on her. And she's at that age where it humiliates her to have to admit in public that she has a father.

I thought about calling Wayne again, and then remembered I still hadn't done my readings. He was sure to ask about that, so I dug my books out and read a few pages before I dozed off.

Miss Missouri's knocking on the door woke me half an hour later. She held Billy Bob in her arms and he was looking cranky.

"He's yours," she said, handing him over. "He wants to eat, but you better clean him up first."

She glanced down gloomily at a damp spot on her blouse where Billy Bob had been resting against her body.

"Sorry 'bout that, Miss Missouri," I said, taking him in my hands but holding him away from my own clean but faded Rice Owls tee shirt.

"Oh, it'll wash out. Lord knows, I've washed enough baby pee and poop out of my clothes over the years."

She leaned over and patted Billy Bob on the head and left.

I took him into the room he shared with Katie and put him on the changing table. Billy Bob hates being messed and loves being cleaned. You would think that would make it easy to take care of him. But he also thinks getting cleaned is a game and that his job is to keep swatting the damp cloths and all other supplies away, gurgling happily for every score he makes. Before LuNella left, when she did all the baby-tending, I was watching her fool with him one day and asked her if it didn't bother her that he was wriggling around.

"No, it's just a game," she said, smiling down at him with her beautiful eyes.

I tried not to think of LuNella's eyes. When they had looked at me over the last couple of years, they were either filled with tears, dismay or anger.

Once it became my job to clean and change Billy Bob, I found myself getting very angry with him and fighting him to stay still. This just made him wriggle all the harder. Then I remembered what LuNella had said and changed my attitude. I knew I could get this done faster if he would just cooperate. But what else did I have to do? And why was I in a hurry to get away from my little boy?

Miss Missouri's words about Katie echoed in my head: "Trust me, she will be growing up way too fast, way too soon."

I gazed down at Billy Bob.

"You, too, kid. You, too."

I checked to see his diaper was secure, tugged his little pants up and lifted him to my shoulder.

"Ready for some creamed peas? Mmm, good!" I lied through my teeth.

About four o'clock, I heard Katie come in the back door. She was talking to someone and I went to see. Probably Belinda. Those two were BFFs. Whatever that means.

When I walked into the kitchen, Katie had her head in the refrigerator and was alone.

"I thought I heard you talking to someone," I said, kissing the top of her head. "Did Belinda come home with you? I'm making chicken nuggets for dinner, and there'll be plenty if you want her to stay and eat. I can call her mom and make sure it's okay."

I liked Belinda. She was a skinny little thing with copper-wire hair and more freckles than you can shake a stick at. Her father was a lawyer with an office in Davis, and her mother helped with the Baptist Church daycare center. They were nice people, and they had been kind to me when LuNella ran off. Margaret Scranton, Belinda's mother, had brought me a casserole – the small town Texas contribution to all manner of grieving processes -- and told me that Katie could stay with them for a while if I wanted.

I was still in shock and heard her through a drunken haze.

"Sure," I slurred, "maybe jush tonight. She's over at Miss Missouri's."

Of course, that was the night I wound up in jail and the Scrantons wound up keeping Katie for three extra days until I was able to come home. As grateful as I was that they took care of Katie while Miss Missouri was taking care of Billy Bob, I was even more grateful that when I came to pick Katie up to take her home, Margaret had just given me a hug and said, "It'll be all right, Corny. It'll be all right."

No lecture, no pious Bible verse. Just a hug and simple encouragement.

I picked up the phone to call to invite Belinda to stay, but Katie stopped me.

"Oh, it's not Belinda. Her folks are taking her and Toby to a movie tonight and she had to get home to eat early. No, it's the boy. He's in the bathroom."

The boy. The bathroom?

I looked down the corridor just in time to see the door to the guest bathroom open and the boy come out.

He was just under five feet tall, I would guess. From the bottom of his bare feet, pale with dust, to the top of his head of dirty blond hair, that is. The wings reached another foot above that, white, not glowing. Just white. Normal white, like bird wings. As he came closer, I saw that he had green eyes, no, maybe hazel. He had a light tan and what looked like a downy hint of stubble on his chin. He was wearing what I assumed were the same cargo pants Katie had described, worn but not torn. The many pockets didn't sag, so I guess he wasn't carrying anything in them. He was bare-chested, but he had on a nondescript vest.

I backed up until I hit the wall. I was still holding the phone and it was a moment or two before I realized that the annoying buzz I heard was not in my head but the phone signaling that it was off the hook. I fumbled trying to put it back on the stand and managed after three tries.

The boy smiled and came closer, his hands in his pockets. He didn't say anything, but he cocked his head to the side and peered at me. He didn't look afraid or curious or … anything, really. He was just there.

In my kitchen.

With his white wings.

How did he get the vest on over the wings? I found myself wondering foolishly. As if that was the important question.

"Daddy," Katie said, ever polite and as if this was the most natural thing in the world, "this is Angelo. I told you about him."

Automatically I stepped forward and held out my hand.

Angelo looked at it for a moment and then at Katie.

"This is my daddy. Shake his hand, silly," she said.

He reached out and took my hand, turned it over and looked at it closely for a moment, then looked up and grinned, shaking it vigorously up and down.

I was still is a daze and just stood there while he pumped my arm like he was working an old well pump.

"That's enough," Katie laughed, and Angelo let go.

"Hello, Angelo," I said. "Welcome to our home?"

He nodded and looked around the room. I just kept staring at him, trying to keep my eyes on his face and not on the wings. My eyes kept drifting over his shoulder, though, where the wings moved slightly. He caught me looking and, with a sly look, moved the wings a bit more. He gazed around the room and moved into the very center. Suddenly he spread the wings their full expanse, reaching almost from wall to wall. I jumped back, startled, and reached instinctively for Katie and pulled her close.

She leaned into my side, her eyes on the boy with his amazing wings, and asked calmly, "Can Angelo stay for dinner?"

I nodded. And then I was struck by an awful thought.

"Uh, we're having chicken. Do you think … will that be okay?"

"I guess so," she said. "Why?"

I didn't want to say that for a moment I wondered if he might be related or something. I mean, those wings and …

I was getting more confused by the moment. This was such a strange turn of events, but everything felt the same. The kitchen was the same, when I looked out the window, the back yard was the same, the scrub oaks in the field behind the house were the same. Off in the distance, I could see the edge of town. The same old Blakesfield.

And there was a boy with wings standing in my kitchen, waiting to see if he could stay for dinner.

"Well, honey," I said to Katie, trying to make my voice as normal as it was likely to be under the circumstances. "Angelo is welcome, but you know, if he's going to stay for dinner, we better let his parents know."

He had parents, I assumed. I mean, he came from somewhere.

Where did he come from? Did his parents have wings? Was I drunk?

"Katydid, sweetie, would you do Daddy a favor and pinch me?"

She pulled away and looked at me.

"I know what you're thinking, you goose," she said, "but it's not a dream."

"Pinch me anyway," I said firmly, and my obedient daughter did so.

I did not wake up.

"Hey," she called to Angelo, "want to meet Billy Bob?"

They headed to the back of the house.

Mechanically I checked the chicken tenders soaking in the sink to see if they had thawed. Close enough, I thought. I went to the cabinet for the biscuit mix and found myself wondering what Angelo ate.

Did we have any sunflower seeds?

Shoot, I told myself, reaching to the top shelf for the mix, *maybe he's related to the chicken hawks and this will be right up his alley.*

Talking to yourself now, are you? You need to call Wayne.

I put the biscuit mix box down on the counter and turned to the phone. It rang just as I reached for it.

"Wayne?" I asked, my voice rising hopefully.

"No, Corny, it's me," said Missouri's voice. "I just wanted to warn you. Wanda Mae's headed over there."

Wanda Mae?

"Why?" I asked but the front doorbell rang before I got an answer. "She's here. Talk to you later."

I hung up and went to the front.

Wanda Mae was standing there, a foil-covered paper plate in her hands. She peered over my shoulder, talking a mile a minute.

"Why, hi, Corny! I was over at my sister's with this sweet potato pie and I thought I might bring you a couple or three pieces. Did you ever eat any of my sweet potato pie? Edd Earl used to say it was the best he ever ate, and I took that as a real compliment because you know his mama, Miss Edna, was a real good cook and Edd Earl was used to the best."

I knew I should invite her in, but I wasn't sure when Katie and Angelo might reappear.

"Why, thank you, Miss Wanda Mae, that's mighty sweet of you. I never had any of Miss Edna's food myself, but I always did hear tell that she was one of the best cooks in Windham County."

Actually what I had heard was that she was one of the fattest and nosiest, but I saw no need to make waves.

I reached for the pie and stood in the doorway, trying to block the view.

Wanda Mae kept talking but never looked me in the face, her eyes darting from side to side.

"Well, this one here is real good, if I do say so myself. I make it with real sweet potatoes, you know, not with those canned things. And I use those big marshmallows and cook it until they are just turning brown. Mmm, mmm, is it ever sweet? How are y'all doing? I'm ashamed I haven't been over to see you more since …"

Her voice died out and she looked confused for a moment. Then she put on a bright face.

"But I'm here now, ain't I?"

She stepped back and gave me the once over.

"You're looking good, Corny. I think you've lost weight. Must be all that bicycle riding you've been doing. I see you on that bike all the time. Are Katie and Billy Bob okay?"

I shifted on my feet and tried not to look over my shoulder.

"Well, Miss Wanda Mae, they're all fine."

"I'd love to say hi to Katie and kiss that baby," she said, putting a foot forward.

I didn't move.

"Well, I know they'd like that, but I'm … I'm cooking chicken for dinner and I have to get back to the kitchen before it burns the house down. Maybe next time. Thanks again for the pie. It will make supper that much better, I know that. Bye now."

This time it was Wanda Mae who didn't move.

"I could swear I saw Katie come in with someone a little while ago. I didn't see who it was, but it didn't look like anyone from around here."

"Yeah, some new friend. I just met him myself. I really have to go. I'll talk to you later, Miss Wanda Mae."

It was the bum's rush, and I knew a dark version of my behavior would be all over Blakesfield and surrounding areas before the night was out. But I didn't know what else to do, and I stepped back inside and closed the door carefully.

Miss Wanda Mae sniffed loudly and called, "Well, goodbye to you, Corny Shane!"

I went back into the kitchen and found a clear spot on the counter to set the sweet potato pie. I unwrapped it and looked at it. It did look pretty appetizing, and I picked up a piece that had fallen off a corner and put it in my mouth. As advertised, it was sweet indeed.

When I went back to the sink and looked out the back window, I saw Wanda Mae had gone back to her car the long way, circling around the house and glancing in each window she passed. I could only hope Katie and Angelo were not in view.

Not in view? That might not be good.

"Katie, Angelo!" I shouted down the hall. "I need to talk to you."

A moment later they were back in the kitchen.

"Um, I never really got an answer about Angelo's parents. Do you have a phone number where I can call them?"

Katie looked at him. He looked back.

"Do you have a phone at home?" she asked.

He cocked his head but his expression did not change.

"You know," she pointed to our phone, "a telephone. Or maybe a cell phone?"

He looked away, seeming to lose interest.

She looked at me and shrugged.

I gave it a shot. I went and stood right in front of him.

"Angelo," I said, "you are welcome to eat with us, but I need to tell your parents where you are. I don't want them to worry about you. Understand?"

He looked at me with those clear hazel eyes, but he gave no indication of understanding, certainly no sign he was going to respond.

"He doesn't talk," Katie told me.

"Does he hear?" I asked, keeping my eyes on his face.

"I think so. When people shout or if there is a loud noise, he looks that way. But he never says anything."

"How did you find out his name then?" I asked, turning to my daughter

"Oh, that's just what Belinda and I decided to call him. Because he looks like an angel and it's a boy's name. Maybe it is his name."

"Oh? Why do you say that?"

"When I call him Angelo, he looks at me."

What if you have called him Big Bird? I wondered.

"Big Bird," I said, but he didn't look toward me.

"Daddy!" Katie cried. "Don't be mean!"

I blushed.

"Sorry. I was just trying something. I didn't mean anything by it."

"Come on, Angelo," she said, taking him by the hand, "let's go outside and sit on the swings."

They went out the back door, Katie casting a reproving glance in my direction. It made her look even more like LuNella. My ex used to look at me like that a whole lot.

Now what? I asked myself.

Chapter 8

I picked up the phone and called Wayne. It went to voice mail and I left a message. Then I called Miss Missouri.

"Missouri here," she answered.

"Miss Missouri, it's me," I said. "Can I come over for a minute?"

"Sure thing. I'm just putting a chicken pot pie in the toaster oven, but those things take forever and I got plenty of time. Come on."

"Thanks, I'll be right there. I won't stay long. I have to get supper in the oven."

"Okay. Oh, and Corny?"

"Yes?"

"I'm looking out my kitchen window at your swing set. You know what I mean?"

Her phone clicked off.

I knew what she meant.

When I got to her house, Miss Missouri was sitting in a wrought iron bistro chair beside a table on her glassed-in porch, looking out at Katie and Angelo on the swings.

"She brought him home for dinner," I said, sitting down in the chair on the other side of the table. I shifted it so that I could see the swing, too.

"Hmm," she said and turned to me, smiling.

"Miss Missouri, I don't know what to make of this."

I threw my hands up in the air. She gazed at me but didn't answer.

"Aren't you bothered by that … that thing out there with the wings?" I asked.

She shook her head and looked back at the kids.

"He's beautiful, don't you think. I don't mean pretty or even handsome. Just beautiful. The wings just look natural on him, like they just grew there."

She laughed and went on, “Well, I guess they *did* just grow there.”

“I don’t see why you are so calm about this. It’s weird. Too weird.”

“Oh, Corny! If you had taught school as long as I did, you wouldn’t think anything was too weird.”

Katie and Angelo were swinging in sync. She was pushing off with her feet, going higher and higher. His feet swung free, but his wings flapped gently from time to time, keeping the two of them side by side. She was chattering away as usual. His face was turned away from me toward her, but I knew he was silent. Just listening.

“This isn’t some odd little quirk in one of your students, Miss Missouri. He has wings. Wings!”

Miss Missouri looked at Katie’s face and murmured, “I know. Ain’t it grand.”

I sputtered and was trying to formulate an answer when my cell phone started playing “Friends in Low Places.” Wayne.

“’Scuse me for a moment, okay?” I said, getting up and walking out the side door and back into the summer heat.

“Okay, I’m on break,” Wayne was saying into my ear, “and this better be important. I need to pee something bad.”

“Can’t you pee and talk at the same time? You got, whaddayacallit, one of them shy bladders?” I teased.

“I ain’t got no shy nothin’, but I sure cain’t hold no phone to my ear and unzip my pants and … Just talk. Time’s a wastin’.”

“Look,” I said, “you go pee. I’m talking to Miss Missouri right now. Call me on your next break.”

“Okay. There’ll be a lull around eight. I’ll call then.”

We clicked off and I went back to Miss Missouri.

“Sorry about that. It was Wayne returning a call.”

“Wayne helping you with things, huh. Is that working out?” she asked, not looking at me.

“Yeah, he’s helping a lot.”

“What does he say about this?” she asked.

"Well, he hasn't heard the latest. When I told him what Katie said yesterday, he took it in stride. He told me not to get tied up in knots over it."

"Sounds like good advice to me. Accept the things you cannot change, isn't that what you folks say? This sure looks like something you can't change. Looks like it to me, that is."

I sighed.

"I reckon you're right."

"You know what you can do, though?" she asked.

"What?"

"You can go cook those kids some supper."

I nodded, got up and headed back to the kitchen.

After I got the chicken nuggets in the oven, I went to get Billy Bob ready. He was sitting up and watching the mobile hanging over his bed. I picked him up and rested him on my left arm, felt his bottom with my right hand to make sure he was dry and went back to the kitchen. I got him settled in his high chair and put a handful of oat cereal on the tray for him to eat or play with. It was even odds which it would be. He grabbed a fistful and waved it in the air before throwing it at me and bursting into giggles.

"Stop that," I said, smiling.

He grabbed another fistful and threw it.

"Okay, buster," I said, sweeping the fallen pieces up with my hand and dropping them into the trash. "That's it."

He looked me in the face and moved his hand toward the tray. I looked stern and said, "No."

He never broke eye contact and put his fist down and grabbed more of the cereal.

"No, Billy Bob. No."

He looked directly at me, lifted his fist and put the cereal in his mouth.

"You little booger," I laughed, kissing him on top of his head.

The oven bell rang and I took the nuggets out. I got a big plate out of the cabinet, slid the nuggets onto the plate, pulled the ketchup bottle out of the refrigerator for Katie and Angelo and the barbecue sauce out of the microwave for me. I put everything on the table and went to the back door.

"Katie! Angelo! Dinner's ready."

Katie came to the door alone.

"Where's Angelo?" I asked, looking toward the swing.

"He flew off," she said. "Just like yesterday. We were swinging and then he just got down, waved at me and ran toward the driveway. Before he got there, he spread his wings and flew off toward the lake."

Toward the lake. Maybe tomorrow Wayne and I could go check out the lake.

"Well, you come in and eat while the food's still hot," I said, closing the door behind her.

We had a quiet dinner. Billy Bob was on his best behavior, ate more cereal and some of the creamed spinach that the pediatrician swore was good for him and that I thought looked like it had already been through him once.

"Get him used to eating it when he's young, and he'll eat it the rest of his life," Dr. Sashan told me. "Develop good habits early."

Whatever.

I cut the sweet potato pie into four pieces, put Katie's slice on a saucer and mine on my plate. She looked at me. We didn't have sweets very often. I wished we had some whipped cream to go with it.

"Miss Wanda Mae brought it," I told her.

She cut off a piece with her fork, put it in her mouth and smiled.

"That's good pie!" she said after she had swallowed. "I love sweet potato pie. Why don't you make pies, Daddy?"

I swallowed the mouthful I had and said, "I don't know how. And you don't need to eat anymore sugar than you already do, young lady."

Billy Bob interrupted us. He banged on the tray on his high chair and held his arms out to me.

"What do you want, buddy?" I asked, turning in my chair to face him.

"Pah … pah … pah," he said, screwing up his face.

I was stunned.

"Katie! I said, he just called me Papa. He talked and he called me Papa!"

She looked at me with pity.

"I'm pretty sure he was just asking for pie."

"No, he … Really? You think he just wants pie?"

She nodded.

I got my spoon and scooped up a bit of filling, making sure not to get any of the melted marshmallows. Once he got that stuff on his face, I would never get it clean.

"Pah … pah!" he said happily and I put the spoon to his lips. He opened his mouth and I maneuvered the orange mush into his mouth. He closed his mouth, burbled a little bubble out his lips and swallowed. He rewarded me with a beatific smile.

"Well," I said, disappointment ringing in my ears, "at least he said a word. Even if it was pie."

Katie laughed.

"That's okay, Daddy. He loves you, even if he doesn't know how to say Dada or Papa or anything yet."

I left Billy Bob in his high chair so he could watch me and Katie do the dishes. He was fascinated by the water running out of the faucet and stretched his hands out toward it. I kept saying, "Water, water," trying to get him to say another word, but I had no luck. For now my son's vocabulary consisted of one word and one word only: pie.

We had just finished the dishes and I was getting him cleaned and ready for bed when the doorbell rang.

I looked at the clock. It was just after seven. Not late, but then we seldom had unexpected company at night.

"Katie," I called, "could you see who's at the door, please. Tell them I'm busy with Billy Bob, but I'll be there right away."

"Yes," she shouted back.

An idea occurred to me.

"Katie, wait. Look through window and see who it is before you open the door."

There was a moment's pause and I waited, ear cocked.

"It's just Miss Smithers," she said.

Joanne Smithers was the pastor at Evangel Temple. I wondered why she was there. Asking for money, most likely. Or trying to get me to come to her church. Well, she was harmless, anyway. At least I guessed she was.

"Okay, let her in. Tell her I'll be right there. And see if she wants some sweet tea."

I got Billy Bob settled, wound up the mobile and set it turning, switched on the night light, made sure the baby monitor was turned on, kissed my son and went out the door, turning off the overhead light and pulling the door partway shut.

Joanne Smithers was sitting in the living room, a glass of sweet tea on a tray on the small table beside her chair. She started to get up when I came in, but I waved her back to her seat.

"Hey, Joanne," I said.

We had been in school together, but we had never been particularly close. Like I said, she seemed harmless but she was a professional church lady. You never knew.

"Corny," she said. "I was hoping to speak with you about something."

She looked meaningfully at me, then at Katie, then back at me. I took the hint.

"Katie, honey," I said, "why don't you go out back and play while it's still light so Miss Smithers and I can talk."

Katie hopped up from the couch where she was sitting and went out without a word.

"Okay, I'm all ears. What's up?"

"I hear you had company today," she said.

News travelled fast. I guess Wanda Mae had been busy.

"Company?"

"I heard Katie brought someone home with her from the park."

"Oh, him. Yeah. He's a new friend. Angelo. Nice kid. Quiet type. You gotta like that."

She waited for me to go on.

"Well, Corny, who is he?" she demanded.

I shrugged and pretended more indifference than I felt.

"I don't know. I just met him for the first time this afternoon. Katie brought him home for dinner, but it sounds like you already knew that. I asked him who his parents were, but he never got around to telling me. So that's all I know. He went home before dinner, and I didn't have a chance to find out any more."

"I heard," she said slowly and paused meaningfully, "that he has wings."

I thought about it for a minute. I was getting irritated.

"Well, now that you mention it, I suppose he did. Have wings, that is. Nice white ones."

"Doesn't that bother you?"

It did bother me, but I was not going to let her know that. I was beginning to feel like my private space was being trampled.

"I try not to let things bother me, Joanne. There must be something in the Bible about that. Not worrying and so on. And something about entertaining angels unaware. Maybe that's what I was doing. Entertaining an angel unaware and all."

That stumped her for a moment, but she regrouped.

"How do you know he wasn't something else. St. Paul says in Second Corinthians that Satan disguises himself as an angel of light. How do you know that wasn't Satan sitting at your dining table?"

"Well, first off, as I already told you, he went home before dinner, so whoever he was, he wasn't sitting at my dining table. And second, why would I think he was Satan? It was just a kid. Nothing of fire and brimstone about him."

"A kid? Where did he come from? Where did he go when he left? Who is he?"

"I told you," I said, my voice growing icier by the moment. "I don't know. For all I know he's a hobo, a tramp, a vagabond, a landloper."

I could tell that *landloper* reference threw her off her stride. Besides my degrees in philosophy, I had a graduate degree in English. When I couldn't find a job, I just kept going to school.

See, Wayne, I thought smugly, *sometimes those six-bit words come in handy.*

"I'm just not comfortable with this," she finally said.

I realized she sounded a lot like I had sounded just a few hours ago.

I tried to be polite.

"I can see that, Joanne, but I don't think you need to worry. After all, he came here for dinner, not to your house. There's nothing for you to feel comfortable or uncomfortable about."

"We need to find out something, Corny," she went on. "A woman doesn't feel safe with strange people about."

"I admit it's strange, Joanne," I said, attempting to calm her down by keeping my own voice soft and even. "But there is no sign that he is a danger. Katie is certainly not afraid of him."

She looked at me sharply.

"Katie is a child. Your child, and it is up to you to protect her from danger, not to let her wander into it willy-nilly. Open your eyes, Corny! Who knows who or what this thing is. It might be … you know, something evil."

She had leaned forward while saying this, but she paused and leaned back to see how I reacted.

Fool woman! I thought, but I held my tongue. I had never noticed any fool becoming less foolish when their foolishness was pointed out. And Joanne apparently was the worst kind of fool in my book, one who thought her foolishness was the wisdom of God.

"I'm sorry, Joanne," I said, still trying to be polite. "I don't know any more than I have told you. I assure you I am not concealing anything. I don't know where Angelo came from or where he went when he left. I saw nothing while he was here that would make me think he is an instrument of Satan, much less Satan himself come to Blakesfield, of all places. Let's not get carried away."

She reached for her purse and stood up. For the first time I realized she had been clutching a Bible in her hand the whole time. She shook it in my face.

"You'll see, Corny Shane! Bad company corrupts! It says so in the Bible. You should keep your daughter away from that thing. He's bad company. I'm as sure of it as I am that Jesus is my Lord!"

I stood, too.

"Well, Joanne, you are sure of more things than I am. But I imagine you need to get back to searching the scriptures for more wisdom."

"You make fun, Corny Shane, you make fun! You with all your family's money and all your fancy degrees. None of that kept you from becoming a …"

I flushed bright red and she stammered before going on.

"But the day will come, as it comes to all, when you have to stand before the judgement seat of God almighty and give an account of yourself. What will you say then?

I'm not much of a Bible scholar, but a verse popped into my head.

"I don't know. Maybe I can say, I saw you a stranger with wings, and took you in."

At that her own face flooded with red and she sputtered, gripping the Bible so tightly her knuckles whitened..

"The devil can quote scripture, Corny. That don't prove anything!"

My phone rang. Probably Wayne, I hoped.

"Good night, Joanne," I said, moving toward the door and holding it open.

She stormed out into the darkness. I waited until I heard her start her car and saw her back out and turn down Southwood Drive, heading toward the Farm to Market Road before I closed the door. By then the land line had stopped ringing. Thirty seconds later my cell phone gave forth with "Friends in Low Places."

"Wayne, man, thanks. I just had the strangest visit from Joanne –"

When I turned around, Katie was standing in the living room, holding her calico cat, Sweet Thing.

"Angelo's not Satan, Daddy," she said. "He's not!"

"Wayne," I said, "I'm sorry. I'll have to call you back. A little situation here."

"Whatever," he said, clicking off.

I put my arm around Katie and pulled her to me.

"I know, honey. I know. But adults, well, sometimes adults are afraid of things they don't understand."

I should know. I was one of them.

"She sounded so hateful," Katie sniffed. "And she's a preacher. Preachers aren't supposed to be hateful."

I hugged her tighter and Sweet Thing growled.

"She's not hateful, Katie. I've known Joanne Smithers since we were little, and she's a lot of things. But she's not hateful. She's just confused and afraid"

I waited until the sniffling died down and then whispered.

"You know why she's scared, don't you?"

Katie shook her head against my chest.

"Angelo's not scary. He's nice. I like him."

"Well, snookums, you know Angelo, don't you? You've played with him and you even invited him home with you. And you took him to meet Billy Bob. You know he's not scary. But Joanne doesn't know him. Far as I know, she hasn't even seen him herself. She just heard about him. And all she heard was that he's a stranger. Not just a stranger, but strange because he has wings. And for some people, especially for people who spent their whole lives here in Blakesfield and consider a trip to Austin a big adventure, everything and everyone who is strange is scary."

I held her out at arm's length and she looked at me. Sweet Thing struggled to get out of her grip and jumped to the floor. The cat looked back at me with her blank face.

Katie calls her Sweet Thing because she could never make up her mind what to name the kitten Miss Missouri gave her for her birthday three years ago. She just called it a sweet thing for so long that Sweet Thing became the kitten's name. To Katie she was still Sweet Thing. For some reason, the cat had never had any use for me. Maybe that was why I just called it Thing.

I looked back at my daughter's face, smudged with dust and tears.

"Remember when that policeman came to your school last year and talked to you about being careful around people you didn't know, people he called strangers?"

She nodded and chanted, "Stranger danger! Stranger danger!"

"Well, lots of people think all strangers are a danger."

"But that's kid stuff," she said, "not for grownups. Grownups shouldn't be afraid. They're big. They're grown up."

"Well, a lot of grownups are still little inside. I think maybe Joanne is like that, she's still a scared little girl inside. Maybe ..."

Maybe, I thought, *that's why she got religion.* But I wasn't going to get into that discussion with an eleven-year-old.

"Anyway, we won't worry about it. Maybe she'll go home and think about it and tomorrow she'll feel different. You'll see. Things aren't as scary in the morning light. Not even boys with wings, maybe."

She looked past me through the windows. In August, it was still light outside. I saw the look on her face but chose to ignore it.

I could always hope, right?

Chapter 9

That night I dreamed of flying. In the dream, I didn't have wings like Angelo's. I was in a house, a two-story house, and I flew out of my room on the second floor and down the stairs. I sort of glided, guiding myself by touching the wall and the stair railing. I turned and continued down the hall, just sort of hanging in the air, almost like I was always falling but never touching down. I wasn't sure how long I could do it, how long it would take before my feet touched the ground. There was nothing scary about the dream. It wasn't one of those dreams where you are falling and falling in a bad way. It was quite nice.

I remember learning in physics that in a certain sense, planets and other objects in solar orbit can be said to be falling toward the surface of the sun but that they are falling at such a speed and such an angle that they keep falling ahead and circle around and around. That was what flying was like in my dream. I was falling but I was never going to hit the ground as long as I kept pushing myself ahead by pushing off on walls and other things.

There was no story to the dream. Just flying. And a feeling of incredibly security and ease. I woke up more refreshed than I had been since LuNella left.

Everything's going to be fine, I told myself in the mirror while I brushed my teeth.

I went to get Katie up and check on Billy Bob. I was grateful that he slept through the night and had not reached the stage where he tried to climb out of his crib. He was still asleep, his little chest rising and falling. I watched him for a while.

"Why didn't you say Papa?" I whispered.

I imagined him opening his eyes and saying, "I did. I didn't say *pie*. I said *Papa*."

"I knew it," I said out loud and left the room

Katie had already poured her bowl of cereal and started eating when I got to the kitchen. I got a frozen breakfast sandwich out of the freezer, wrapped it in a paper towel and put it in the microwave. While I waited for the sandwich to cook, I studied my daughter.

Katie is a pretty little thing. I know, every parent thinks that their kid is beautiful and the older I get, the more I realize that every kid is beautiful. But Katie had a lot of her mother's looks, and LuNella was a beautiful woman.

When she and Hank and I were seniors at Cherokee Creek High, the only kids from Blakesfield in our class, we ruled the place. Hank was my best friend back then and a great athlete. He led the Cherokee Creek Warriors to the State Six-Man Football Championship game that year, and he always claimed they had been robbed of the championship itself by a bad referee call that invalidated a last minute touchdown. He was so angry when we got back from Austin that weekend that I took him out and got him drunk for the first time in his life.

Needless to say, it wasn't my first time or my last. It wasn't Hank's last time either. Unfortunately.

He was the jock and I was the brain. LuNella was smart, too, smart and beautiful. She was head cheerleader, homecoming queen, editor of the yearbook. She and I fought for top grades in every class and I beat her out for valedictorian by less than a hundredth of a point. She and Hank were an item all through high school and everyone expected them to get married. But that's not what happened.

But I'll tell you about that later.

That morning at breakfast I saw LuNella's reflection in Katie and my heart ached. I hoped no boy ever treated Katie as badly as I had treated her mother.

"Katie?" I asked.

She was eating some awful colored sugary cereal and reading the back of the box. Does every kid in America read cereal boxes?

"Hmm?" she responded without taking her eyes off the box.

"What do you and Angelo do when you're at the park?"

She took her eyes off the box and focused on me.

"We play. You know, kid stuff. We swing and we run around and play tag with Belinda and Toby and Hank and whoever's there. Just the regular stuff."

She lost interest and turned her attention back to the cereal box.

"And we talk," she said quietly.

"What do you mean, y'all talk? I thought he didn't talk."

She put another spoonful of cereal in her mouth and kept reading.

"Katherine Nell Shane, look at me. I thought you said Angelo didn't talk"

She pushed the box away and turned sideways in her chair just as the microwave bell rang. I turned around and took the warm sandwich out of the machine, unwrapped the paper towel and tossed it in the trash can. I sat down at the table and placed the sandwich on a napkin to cool.

"I'm waiting," I said.

"Well, I talk and he listens. And then … I don't think he talks in my head exactly, but I kind of hear myself saying things I didn't know before."

"Like what kind of things?"

"Like the other day, I was upset with Billy Bob and I was complaining about him. And I went on and on, and Angelo just looked at me and listened. Finally I ran down and stopped talking. We walked about a block and then I heard myself saying, 'Well, he's just a baby really. And he don't have a Mama. And Daddy does all he can, but I guess I could help more. Maybe … Maybe Billy Bob isn't always trying to get Daddy's attention. Maybe sometimes he's just wet himself.'"

"And what did Angelo do?"

She grinned.

"He didn't do anything. He just looked at me that way he does and nodded a little."

"Well, you know Billy Bob is a baby. What part didn't you know already?"

"I guess I never really thought about what that meant. I sort of thought, well, didn't think exactly, but I just thought Billy Bob was just a little me. That he knew the things I know, that he knows why … why Mama's not here," she looked away, "and why sometimes you can't get out of bed, and …"

My eyes teared up and I looked down at the table. To cover the awkward silence, I picked up my sandwich and bit into it. I chewed for a while, decided I was okay and swallowed.

"Katie, it's been a long time since I couldn't get out of bed. A long time!"

She wrinkled her eyes.

"I know. And I know you're trying, I really do. But Billy Bob, he doesn't know anything, does he? He's just a baby. So I guess the part I didn't know was what it was like to be a baby and not know nothing."

She went back to her cereal box, finished reading the back and turned it so she could read the side. I was just finishing my sandwich when I heard Billy Bob starting to wake up.

I headed back to take care of Billy Bob and Katie called after me.

"Don't forget Vacation Bible School starts today."

I had been raised Catholic, but I gave up on that a long time ago. Like most adolescents, I went through a rebellious atheist stage. Unlike most of them, I never completely recovered. Some people in AA say they are "recovering Catholics." It sounds clever but I don't like to hear it. I can understand what they mean, but I don't ever hear anyone say, "I'm Roscoe and I'm a recovering Presbyterian." Maybe Presbyterians don't recover.

At any rate, LuNella and I had a Catholic wedding, but neither one of us was religious. When Katie was born we didn't have her baptized, although our parents nagged us about it. LuNella would have gone along with them just to get them off our backs, but I was stubborn and refused. I remember one drunken fight about it that I got into with both sets of parents at Katie's first birthday party. I wound up throwing the cake on the floor and threatening to pour beer on her head and baptize her myself. I wish I could say I was in a blackout, because then I wouldn't remember the looks on everyone's faces. Unfortunately I remembered very well.

And I used to wonder why my ex-laws and my own parents didn't want to have much to do with me! Now that I've been sober a few twenty-four hours, I wonder instead why LuNella didn't pack her bags and take Katie then and there and go home to her parents.

Anyway, I still didn't go to church, but Katie went to Bible Baptist because that's where Belinda and her family went. I used to drive her over there Sunday mornings and they would bring her home. Now that I couldn't drive, they came and got her. They were good people and acted like it was the most natural thing in the world to drive across town to pick up a little girl, then turn around and drive back to take her to church while her alcoholic father sat at home and stared at the wall.

Vacation Bible School was one week of Sunday school every day, as far as I could tell. It ran from ten to twelve each day, the kids had lessons and made things out of popsicle sticks and white glue and glitter, learned songs that helped them memorize the books of the Bible and that sort of thing. It ended with a big picnic in Peck's Park. In a place like Blakesfield, it was the highlight of the summer for some of the kids. Several churches used to have Vacation Bible Schools, but in recent years the shrinking population made them decide it was better to co-operate rather than compete for participants.

Each of the five churches in town hosted one day's program. It was the closest thing to the ecumenical movement that our community had to offer. The rest of the year, the kids went to their own Sunday schools and churches and listened to what was wrong with all those other Christians worshipping next door or across the street.

"Okay. How are you going to get there? Is Mrs. Scranton going to come get you?"

"No, I'm going to go with Miss Missouri. It's at the Church of Christ today."

That made life simple.

I picked Billy Bob up, felt around to see how wet he was, grimaced and walked over to the changing table. Several minutes later, I walked back into the kitchen and plopped him into his high chair.

"I want to talk to Miss Missouri about something anyway," I said to Katie while I looked at the tiny jars of baby food to see what Billy Bob was going to get for breakfast. I pulled out a container of apple cinnamon oatmeal. "I'll walk over there with you. When do you need to go?"

"It starts at ten but Miss Missouri likes to be there early. I probably should be at her house before 9:30."

"Okay," I said, distracted by my son's efforts to bat away the spoon filled with oatmeal. "Just let me know and I'll go with."

She rinsed her cereal bowl and spoon and put them in the dishwasher. Billy Bob twisted to look when Katie turned on the faucet and I missed his mouth with the spoon. Apple cinnamon oatmeal dripped down onto his bib.

"Hey, buddy! Pay attention here," I said, grabbing a damp cloth to wipe his face.

He must have thought it was a game because he banged on his tray and grinned widely, displaying about a dozen tiny teeth. I stuck out my tongue at him and he gaggled with delight.

"Pah … pah.. pah," he said.

"Katie," I shouted excitedly, get back in here."

She poked her head around the corner of the door.

"He said Papa, I tell you. Nothing about pie. We weren't even talking about pie."

I turned to him and said, "Say it, Billy Bob, say Papa. Papa. Pah-pah."

He looked blank for a second and then, "Papa."

I hit the table with my palm.

"Plain as day!" I declared, flushed with victory.

Katie rolled her eyes.

"It sure doesn't take much to make you happy," she said and disappeared.

"No, it doesn't," I said, beaming at my son. "You got my brains, kiddo. I can tell already!"

Later I carried Billy Bob in my arms when Katie and I went to Miss Missouri's. I had to brag about how smart he was and tell her he had said Papa.

She stood on tiptoes and kissed him.

"Of course, he's smart. You know, Billy Bob, I taught your daddy and your mama in school and they were two of the smartest kids I ever had in my classroom."

She grinned at me.

"Not the best behaved, however," she sighed.

She looked at Katie, who was shuffling her feet in the brown grass and dried smilax leaves that had blown in from somewhere.

"And your sister," Miss Missouri said, "is smart, too. You come from good stock. Both of you."

"Katie," I said, "you forgot your Bible. Go back to the house and get it while I talk to Miss Missouri for a minute. Hurry!"

Katie ran back to the house and I turned to my neighbor, who was stroking Billy Bob's hair.

"Miss Missouri, I don't have time to go into all the details and I know you want to get going. But I had a troubling visit from Joanne Smithers last night about … well, you know, about our new friend. It sounded like she might stir up trouble. Could you maybe keep your eyes peeled and your ears to the ground to see if anything is up?"

She made a clicking sound with her teeth and nodded.

"That girl never had any sense. Afraid of her own shadow when she was a kid in my class. You could make her cry just by looking cross-eyed at her. Anyway, she ought to be at the Vacation Bible School this morning with the kids from her church. I'll keep an eye out and see if she's up to anything."

I could see Katie running back, the white Bible with her name in gold letters tucked under one arm. I thanked Miss Missouri for her help and also for giving Katie a ride.

"I'm happy to do it," she said.

She peered at me over her eyeglasses for a moment.

"You know, Corny, if you ever want a ride to church, my car is big enough for all of us."

I bounced Billy Bob on my hip and shook my head.

"If I ever do, you'll be the first to know," I told her. "But don't hold your breath."

I waved to Katie and walked back to my house.

Chapter 10

Ada, the cleaning lady, came in that morning and I asked her if she would keep an eye on Billy Bob while I went out for a while. He adored her and she was delighted to have the opportunity to ooh and aah with him while the washer and dryer did their duties. I kissed my son on the top of his head and told him to be good.

"Oh," I turned at the door to tell Ada, "he said Papa yesterday."

She beamed almost as much as I had.

Wayne was off on Mondays, because like many eateries, Tiny's was closed on Mondays. I hopped on my bike and rode over to his place in the Paisano Run Mobile Estates. I knew he liked to sleep late on his days off, but it was past ten and surely he was up by then.

I didn't see any lights on when I pulled the bike up to his mobile home, a fairly new park model. I leaned the bike up against the shabby mesquite tree in the front and walked up the wood steps to his front door. I looked at my watch again. Ten fifteen.

I rang the bell and waited. Nothing happened for at least five minutes. His Jeep was pulled up onto the packed dirt at the end of the park model, so I knew he must be home. I was just getting ready to knock when the door opened.

Wayne is not what you would call a sight for sore eyes on his best day. He's a big man, over six feet tall, with big arms covered with tattoos, a barrel chest and a beer belly that sags below the hem of the Dallas Cowboy tee shirts he usually wears. He was rubbing his eyes and yawning, but he didn't look upset.

"I'm sorry to wake you up," I said, but he waved me inside.

"I was awake. I just hadn't gotten moving yet. You want coffee?"

He headed for the little kitchen and pulled down a couple of chipped mugs with the logo of a long-defunct railroad on them.

"Thanks," I said, settling into one of the chairs by the round table.

He made coffee in one of those French press things, one of the many little quirks that didn't seem to fit my idea of who he was. While we waited for the water to boil, he asked what was up.

"I was a little worried when you didn't call back last night," he said, pouring boiling water into the glass pot and then pushing the plunger to the bottom.

I slapped my head.

"I'm sorry, Wayne," I just got all caught up in trying to sort through things with Katie."

While he poured the coffee into the mugs, I told him about Katie bringing the boy home and about Joanne Smithers. He stood listening until I was done and then sat down.

"Do you think Joanne's gonna make trouble?"

"I don't know. I don't think Joanne knows. And to be honest, I don't even know what trouble would be in this situation. I was as upset and confused about this kid as she was until she started butting in. That got me ticked off and suddenly I was his big defender."

He took a long sip, stretched his arms over his head and popped a few joints.

"Funny how that works, isn't it? One minute you want him to disappear, the next you get upset with someone else who just wants the same thing."

"I know," I shook my head. "It's one of my, oh, you know, my whatchamacallits. Character defects."

"Not just yours," he said. "

One of the steps in recovery is to be ready for God to remove all your character defects. I once joked to Wayne that I didn't have any character defects, just charming idiosyncrasies.

"Mm-hmm," he said promptly, "like using humor to avoid dealing with unpleasant realities."

I think I mentioned that the man can be brutal.

"Anyway, I talked to Miss Missouri about the whole thing. She saw the kid, too, when he was at our house, but she's taking it in stride. Or at least, she's taking a wait-and-see attitude. She took Katie to Vacation Bible School this morning and promised to see if she can find out what Joanne's up to. She'll be there with the kids from Evangel Temple."

"And what are you doing in the meantime?"

"I thought maybe you and I could take a ride out to the lake. Katie says when he flies off, he heads that way. Maybe he's staying out there with someone."

"Family? There aren't any cabins out there."

I snorted.

"For all I know he has a damned nest!"

Wayne nodded over his coffee.

"Could be." He put the empty mug down. "You want to go now?"

"If we could. Katie's at Bible School, but she'll be back for lunch. Ada is at the house cleaning and she's watching Billy Bob for me. But she only stays till noon."

We stood up and headed for the door.

"Guess what! Billy Bob said 'Papa' last night. Plain as day. Said it while we were eating and said it again when I was getting him ready for bed."

Wayne smiled.

"Good for him. Is that what he's gonna call you, Papa?"

"I don't know. Katie calls me Daddy and I imagine that's what he'll call me sooner or later. Papa sounds sort of old-fashioned."

He laughed as we climbed in the Jeep.

"At least it's not *Paw*. That's real hick for you. Real *Little House on the Prairie*."

Granger's Lake wasn't far out of town. As Wayne had said, there weren't any cabins but a few broken-down old sheds were scattered around. He and I walked around the lake and looked into all the sheds. There was no sign of recent occupancy, although there were plenty of old beer bottles and other evidence of teenage activities. The good news was that least some of them were practicing safe sex. We didn't find anything like a nest or any indication that anyone was camping out.

"Well, I'd say this is a bust," I told Wayne after forty-five minutes of futile search. "Of course, Katie didn't say he went to the lake, just that he flew off in this direction."

We got in the Jeep and headed back to town. I scanned both sides of the road as best I could, in case Angelo and his family – if he had such a thing – had a camp site somewhere along the route. I didn't see anything, and the countryside was so barren that even a pup tent would have been obvious.

"I have to go grocery shopping at the Push-n-Shove" Wayne said as we pulled back in Blakesfield. The name of the market was Pik-n-Stik, but the locals all called it Push-n-Shove. "You want to come or you want me to drop you at your house?"

"My bike's at your place," I reminded him. "I don't need anything, but I'll go with you and help you carry things. I can get my bike when you go home."

Wayne cooks for a living but when it comes to himself, he is all convenience. He loaded his cart with frozen pizza, rotisserie chicken, sandwich meat and bread.

"No vegetables?" I asked.

"That stuff grows in the dirt," he growled. "I ain't gonna put it in my mouth!"

I laughed.

He picked up two bags of miniature candy bars – "They say alcoholics should always have chocolate on hand," he reminded me – and two packs of sugar free gum. We checked out and headed back to his place. I helped bring in the bags and asked if he planned to go to the meeting in Cherokee Creek that night.

"Sure," he said, opening a package of pimento loaf and getting a jar of mayonnaise out of the refrigerator. "You coming with me?"

I nodded.

"I'll pick you up around five-thirty then," he said and went back to assembling his wholesome lunch.

I didn't even know they still made pimento loaf. What about olive loaf? I wondered if Katie would eat either one.

I was just putting my bike away when Miss Missouri pulled into her driveway. Katie got out of the car, thanked Miss Missouri politely and ran toward me yelling. I waved at Miss Missouri and she shouted, "Talk to you later. I have news.'

"Good or bad?" I shouted back.

"News," she said and went inside her house.

Ada had heard us and was holding the back door open for us.

"Now y'all be quiet," she scolded in a firm whisper. "I fed Billy Bob and just got him to sleep. Don't you go waking that baby up with your carrying on."

Katie and I looked at one another and tried to look repentant, but we just laughed.

Ada pointed a finger at us and we clapped our hands over our mouths.

"Well, I'm leaving, so if you want to deal with a crying baby, it's up to you two."

"Yes'm," we mumbled through our fingers.

When we got into the kitchen, I saw that Ada had a dish towel draped over a plate of sandwiches in the middle of the table.

"Ada," I said, "you didn't have to make lunch for us."

She frowned.

"I was already feeding Billy Bob and I saw that ham sitting in that fridge. I figured you had better eat it soon, so I sliced it up and made some ham salad for you. It wasn't no trouble and it saved me having to throw that ham out next time I come."

Katie opened a cabinet door and pulled out a bag of corn chips.

"Are you going to eat with us, Miss Ada?" she asked, getting down some plates.

Ada shook her head.

"No, I gotta get home. Y'all enjoy that. I'll see you Thursday."

And she was out the door.

The ham salad was delicious and the corn chips were the perfect accompaniment. A ton of salt, of course, but I tried not to think about that.

"How was Vacation Bible School?" I asked between chips.

"It was okay," Katie said, wiping ham salad from the corner of her mouth. "I'm in Miss Missouri's class."

"Well, she taught for a hundred years, so she should be pretty good."

"Hmmm, hmm. She wants everyone to bring a friend tomorrow, too," she said, looking at me out of the corner of her eye.

"She does, does she? Who are you going to ask? I would have thought every kid in Blakesfield was already there. What else is there to do?"

She hopped off her chair and took her plate to the sink.

"Just about everybody is there, I guess. I thought I might invite Angelo."

Of course. Who else?

"Are you sure that's a good idea? I mean, Angelo's not really from around here. Mabye …"

"No, Alison said her cousin Sam is visiting and wanted to know if it was all right for him to come. Miss Missouri said everyone was welcome. They don't have to be from Blakesfield."

A defiant tone had crept into her voice. Before I could say anything more, she went on.

"And even though he maybe didn't used to be from around here, he's here now, isn't he? And the kids at the park all know him. That's more than know Alison's old cousin Sam."

I got up and cleaned the table. I rolled the top of the corn chip bag up, fastened it with a paper clip and put it back in the cabinet. I rinsed my plate and put it in the dishwasher beside Katie's When I raised back up, she was standing in the doorway.

"Can I go to the park?" she asked.

I sighed. There was no reason to deny her request. She went to the park most afternoons. For a moment I thought about telling her I needed her to watch Billy Bob, but that would just postpone the inevitable.

"Okay," I said. "Before you go down there, stop over at Miss Missouri's and tell her I'll be home all afternoon with Billy Bob if she wants to drop in later for coffee or something."

"Thanks," she said and went out the back door.

I went to the kids' room and checked on Billy Bob. He was sleeping soundly. The light on the baby monitor glowed red. I looked down at my son for long minutes.

Papa.

Finally I went to my room, picked up the Big Book and took it to the living room. I had forgotten to do my readings again that morning. I knew Wayne would ask about it on the drive to Cherokee Creek, and I wanted to be able to tell him I had done it.

He would also ask if I had prayed and meditated, but I always hedged on that one. I thought maybe I needed to get through at least the second step and maybe the third before I started any of that stuff.

When I told Wayne I didn't know how to pray or what to pray for, he had laughed.

"At this point, son, all you need to do is say one word when you get up in the morning: 'Help!' And one word when you go to bed at night: 'Thanks!' I think even a college-educated dude like you can manage that simple task."

"But who am I saying that to?" I demanded.

He shrugged.

"Don't matter. Just say it to the universe right now. That'll do."

I had looked at him doubtfully.

"Okay, but what does that do? How does it work?"

He grinned.

"I'll tell you what my first sponsor told me when I asked him how it worked: 'It works just fine.' And it does. Try it. You might be surprised."

I hadn't been surprised, but that was because I hadn't tried it. It didn't make any sense.

Chapter 11

I read in the Big Book until I heard a knock on the back door. I put the book down and went to check. It was Miss Missouri. I opened the door and invited her in.

"Come in out of that heat," I said.

Central Texas in August is awful. Temperatures of 105 are common. I used to wonder how people stood it in the days before everything was air conditioned. I asked my mama once and she told me people just stood it. It was what there was and you took it.

"Of course," she admitted, "when we were outside in the worst of it, we spent as much time as we could in the water and in the shade."

Miss Missouri came in, fanning herself with one of those old cardboard fans that funeral homes in our area still pass out to people at cemeteries for summer burials. The one in her hands had a gaudy print of an angel with white wings that spread all across the fan. The edge was cut to look like feathers. I wondered if that was why she had chosen it. She had quite a collection, having attended many funerals in her 85 years.

"Would you like some sweet tea?" I asked her.

"That would be wonderful," she said, seating herself at the dining room table. "Do you have any lemon?"

I looked but there wasn't a shriveled slice in sight.

"Sorry. I have some lemon juice."

She shook her head.

"No, that's okay. I can't stand that stuff. It makes my teeth stand on end."

I looked at her.

"Do your teeth normally life flat?"

"You know what I mean. It makes 'em tingle. Plain tea will be fine."

I put ice cubes into her glass and poured the tea. I poured some old coffee into a mug and put in the microwave for myself and turned it on. When the bell dinged, I took it out and sat down at the table.

"So, what's the news?" I asked.

She put down her glass and wrapped her hands around it.

"I don't know what to make of it, but I overheard Joanne Smithers talking to Brother Warren. She was doing all the talking and his back was to me, so I don't know what he said or thought. He's usually pretty balanced in my opinion, but Joanne was sure giving him a hard sell. She was saying she thought they ought to get all the ministers together and do something to protect the children from dangerous influences. I thought about going over and butting in, but just then Thelma Perkins came over and dragged Brother Warren off to break up a fight between some boys out back of the church. Joanne tried to hang onto him, but Thelma insisted."

"Was that all?"

"Joanne stood there looking frustrated and then I saw her make a bee-line for Fred Phillips and Langford Hughes. They were standing over by the coffee urn, eating doughnuts. Fred got a panicked look on his face when he saw Joanne coming, and he took out his cell phone like it had rung. But I'm pretty sure he was just making an excuse, because he turned and walked away with it to his ear but he wasn't saying anything. Langford just stood there and Joanne launched into her spiel again. He nodded for a while and then the bell rang for class to start up again."

I pondered.

"So she is trying to stir things up. If she gets all the churches riled up, it could get messy. Surely some of those ministers have enough sense to find out what the boy's like, though, before they go condemning him. They can't all be like Joanne."

Miss Missouri nodded.

"There's the problem. How are they going to find out anything about the boy. He just appears and disappears, from what Katie told me. And she says he can't talk. Or at least, he doesn't talk. Which makes getting any useful information hard, you have to admit. We don't even know where he's from. And around here, where you're from is the first thing people want to know."

I sipped my coffee and made a face. Stale coffee is terrible and hot stale coffee is no better. I pushed the mug away.

"Wayne and I went out to Granger's Lake this morning to look around. Katie said he flew off in that direction. But we couldn't find any sign of him or anyone else staying out there. And I looked on both sides of the road on the way between here and there without seeing anything."

"Where's Katie now?" she asked, finishing up her tea.

"She went to the park. By the way, she plans to invite Angelo to Bible school."

Miss Missouri smiled.

"I wondered if she would. Might not be a bad idea. At least if he shows up at Bible school, it'll give the preachers a chance to look him over. From what I could tell, Joanne makes it sound like he's the very image of the devil. Maybe when they see he's just a kid with wings, they'll take the rest of what she says with a grain of salt."

She stood up to leave.

"Thanks for the tea. Remind Katie I'll give her a ride to Bible school tomorrow. It's at Good Shepherd Methodist."

I got up, too, and went to open the door.

"I'll let her know."

As Miss Missouri started across my back yard, I called her and she turned around.

"What are you going to do if Angelo shows up, too?"

"Well, I told you Corny, my car's big enough for all of us."

She laughed and went back to her house.

After she left, I dumped the coffee out of my mug and the ice out of her glass. I rinsed them both and sat them on a dish towel to drain.

Maybe I should go to the park, I thought. To see if Angelo is there again. See how the other kids reacted to him. I was sure all the kids must have told their parents about the winged boy. I wondered what they were thinking? It was odd that Joanne was the only one who had come to talk to me about it. I would think it would be the main topic of conversation in Blakesfield.

Then I remembered that I didn't have a lot of friends in Blakesfield. Not anymore. Even though I had grown up here and knew everyone, that meant everyone knew me, too. And they all knew about my drinking and how I acted when I was drunk.

I once heard a joke that there are three kinds of drunks: the jocose, the bellicose and the amorose. I was the bellicose. I probably thought I was humorous and flirtatious, but I was just plain mean when I drank.

I never hit LuNella, I swear to God. But I yelled at her and everybody else when I was under the influence. And for too many years, I was under the influence most of the time. I came home from the bars over in Cherokee Creek way too often with a black eye,

LuNella and I hadn't been married long when I woke up and realized that we weren't getting invited to parties. And no one was ever coming to visit. LuNella had her friends, but they never came to our house. As for my friends, the closest thing to friends were the guys at the bars in Cherokee Creek. You know that theme song about that bar in Boston, something about a place where everybody knew you name and they were always glad you came? Everybody knew my name, but no one was glad I came except when I was buying rounds for everyone there. After I had had a few drinks and began to pick fights, they wished I would leave.

Billy Bob chose that moment to wake up and start crying. I headed back to the kids' room and forgot about any trip to the park, at least for the moment.

When Katie got back from the park, she went right to her room and shut the door. I was making dinner and decided to wait and see what was going on. The baby monitor was on and I could hear Katie mumbling to herself and sobbing. This was not going to be good, I told myself.

Dinner was a frozen pizza but I did make a salad to go along with it. Billy Bob was getting some baby yogurt and creamed carrots. I expected my white tee shirt to be several shades of orange by the time I finished feeding him.

Except for the occasional sobs on the monitor, I hadn't heard a peep from Katie before the oven timer buzzed. I pulled the pizza out of the oven and set it down on the stove to cool while I got the salads out and found the salad dressing. I set up Billy Bob's jars on his high chair, ran the pizza slicer across the hot pizza and lifted pieces onto two plates. I put one in front of Katie's chair and called down the hall.

"Dinner! Come and get it!"

A muffled sound came from the back and the door stayed shut.

I went and knocked on the door.

"Katie, are you all right? I'm coming in."

I pushed on the door but it was latched.

Oh, no, I thought. *We're getting to that age.*

"Katie, come on, let me in. It's time to eat and I need to get Billy Bob."

I heard her turn the latch and the door slid open.

"You can get Billy Bob, but I'm not hungry."

I looked at her face. It was blotchy red and she had obviously been crying. Which I knew already because of the monitor, but I thought it better not to remind her that she didn't have as much privacy as she imagined behind that closed door.

Billy Bob was quiet but his face was solemn, as if he had picked up on his sister's mood. I lifted him up and perched him on my right side.

"Come on, big boy. Come to Papa. Say 'Papa.' Say 'Papa.'"

He looked at me with those big eyes and began to chew on his thumb.

"Katie," I said, heading for the door, "come eat something. I made pizza and salad for you."

She lay down on her bed, turned her face to the wall in the best Old Testament manner and just shook her head.

"I'm not hungry," she said again.

"Well, you don't have to eat. It's not that big a pizza. I can probably finish it all myself if I have to. But at least come sit with me at the table. Billy Bob's not much of a talker yet and I want company."

She lay unmoving for a moment and then a deep sigh escaped her. She rolled over and sat up, wiping her eyes.

"I won't be much company," she said, getting up and slouching through the door and down to the kitchen.

No lie, I thought. *Not good company anyway.*

I got Billy Bob in the high chair, gave him a couple of spoonsful of yogurt and fended off his initial attempt to splatter me with creamed carrots. After a few mouthfuls, he settled back.

I poured some dressing on my salad and poked at it with a fork.

"Are you going to tell me what's wrong?" I asked, picking out a black olive and examining it before popping it into my mouth.

"Nothing," she said. "Everything."

I chewed salad and swallowed. I looked at another olive and said, "Well, that covers the options. Which is it, nothing or everything?"

She put her elbows on the table and placed a hand on each side of her face.

"Well, I went to the park and Angelo wasn't there."

That was a surprise.

"He wasn't there when you got there or he never showed up at all?"

"He wasn't there and he didn't show up. I was going to ask him to come to Bible school tomorrow. But he wasn't there. Belinda and I sat on the swings and waited all afternoon. And that Hank Ingram kept coming by and teasing us about losing our new boyfriend.

"He said, 'Look at the little babies, all broken-hearted because their weird friend didn't come out to play. What's the matter, Katie? Did you run him off like you did your mama?'"

Hank Ingram, Junior was sixteen and the son of my former best friend. He was already growing into a strong, strapping young fellow and looked like he was going to be as good a jock as his father had been. The main difference, as far as I could tell, between sixteen-year-old Hank, Jr. and the sixteen-year-old Hank I had known was that Junior was a troublemaker. He bullied a lot of the kids and made a special effort to make fun of Katie. She couldn't understand why.

"I never did anything to him," she told me the first time he tormented her about LuNella. "Why does he say things like that? What's he got against me?"

I knew it wasn't Katie that he hated. I thought he probably hated me. And maybe LuNella. And I knew why.

Chapter 12

Hank's father and I had been friends all through school. He was always a good guy, polite and gentlemanly. The girls all drooled over him, but LuNella was the one for him. They had been a perfect match. The three of us hung out together all the time, double-dating those times I had a girlfriend of my own. We all figured Hank and LuNella would get married right out of high school, unless their parents could convince them to wait until they graduated from college.

Hank was going to go to Texas A&M on a sort of Baptist football scholarship. That combination may strike some people as odd, but football and Jesus go together in Texas like buttermilk and cornbread. LuNella intended to go to A&M, too, to study to become a veterinarian. I was destined for Rice University in Houston, but that was only an hour or so away from College Station. We would be able to get together regularly. I would be Hank's best man when they got married. LuNella would ask one of her sorority sisters – we all assumed she would be in Delta Delta Delta like her mother – to be her maid of honor. That was the plan.

"Plan plans," I heard someone in the program say one night, "not outcomes."

I mentioned that I got Hank drunk after the state championship loss. He had never had a drink before. His father was a deacon at Bible Baptist Church and alcohol was the devil's brew. I, on the other hand, had been sneaking around drinking since I was twelve and discovered where my father hid the key to his liquor cabinet.

My folks didn't drink heavily, but they were Catholic and it was not an issue for them. My father kept a well-stocked bar in his den, but the booze was under lock and key because he didn't trust Ella, our maid. I guess he didn't care about the beer in the refrigerator or Mama's wine in the cellar.

When Richard and I were little and got a cold, my father would unlock the cabinet and get out the whisky. He would pour a little in a saucepan, add honey and lemon juice and heat it up while he stirred in an aspirin. They he would put us to bed and give us a small glass with the warm home remedy.

Richard never liked it, as I recall. I, on the other hand, thought it would be worth having a cold every day of my life if it meant I could have one of those drinks when I went to bed at night. I don't think my parents noticed, but my colds always lasted longer than Richard's and required more attention.

One afternoon when I was twelve, I went into my parents' bedroom to get something. I don't remember what I was looking for, but I opened dresser drawers and closets at random. I opened my father's closet, looked around aimlessly and was closing the door when my sleeve caught on a nail and ripped. I looked at the ragged edge of the rip and immediately began formulating a lie to cover it up, because I was definitely not supposed to be prowling around in my parents' room. I poked my head around the side of the door, trying to locate the nail that had done the damage. There, just inside the door and on the side of the doorframe, a key hung on a nail.

I lifted the key off and examined it. It was small and brass. It didn't look like a house key or a car key. More like something that would fit my mother's jewelry box. I went over to her dresser and tried the lock. The key didn't fit. That lock was for a flat key and the one in my hand had a round shaft. I stood there for a few minutes, tapping it on my thumbnail and trying to figure out what it could possibly be. Just then I heard Ella coming down the hall, singing "Shall We Gather at the River." I put the key back, closed the closet door and stepped out of the room just as she was coming in.

She looked at me suspiciously.

"What you doin' in there?"

"Nothing," I said and walked away.

I could feel Ella's dark eyes boring into my back all the way down the hall, and I was sure she would tell my mother. I dreaded the confrontation but later that afternoon the washing machine overflowed. Ella must have forgotten all about my misadventure in the chaos that ensued. At any rate, my mother never asked me what I had been up to.

A couple of days later, my father sent me to get a book he had left lying on the table in his den. I picked up the book and was heading back to the living room with it when my eyes fell on the liquor cabinet. The light of the afternoon sun glinted off the cut glass, the brass hinges and the lock on the door.

The lock. It was brass and had a round hole for a key. A key like the one in my father's closet.

I took my father his book and went to my own room to think.

The next afternoon my father went to Davis on business. The pecans were not doing well and the collapse of the orchard was not far off, although none of us knew that at the time. My mother went with him to do some clothes shopping and took Richard along to get new shoes. She wanted me to get shoes, too, but I begged off on the grounds that I had promised to go to Granger's Lake with Hank.

Actually I hadn't promised anything, but we had talked about going. My parents thought the world of Hank, convinced that he could do no wrong and that I was safer with him than anywhere else. I waved them goodbye as they drove off in the Lincoln my father had bought my mother when I was born. He had promised to buy her a Lincoln if she had a boy and he kept that promise. I guess in some ways that made me the son of the promise. Almost Biblical.

I waited half an hour after they left to make sure they didn't come back for something. Mama was notorious for forgetting things and hardly ever managed to go anywhere without having to come back to the house two or three times. When I was sure it was safe, I went to the big bedroom in the back of the house, opened the closet door and took the brass key.

It fit perfectly into the lock on the liquor cabinet. I opened the door and looked in at a wonderland.

My father had bottles of whisky, tequila, brandy, rye, small bottles of colorful liqueurs. I took things out one by one and examined them.

There was my old friend, the cold cure. I opened the bottle and took a sip. Unlike the honeyed cure I sipped in bed, this stung my throat and burned all the way down. I gasped and screwed the top back on the bottle, put it back in its place and picked up another one.

I must have spent an hour sorting through the bottles, taking the occasional sip. The last thing I tasted was green crème de menthe, which may have saved me from a beating. I had just put all the bottles back, locked the cabinet door and returned the key to its hiding place when I heard a car pull up.

I ran to the front door and saw Mr. Ingram getting out of his old Ford. Mr. Ingram was Hank's father and worked for my father at the orchard. He rang the doorbell and waited. I steadied myself and opened the door, blinking out into the bright sun. I leaned against the doorjamb casually.

"Hey, Corny," he said. "Your dad home?"

"No sir," I said, enunciating carefully. "They went to Davis. I don't expect them back until late this afternoon."

He frowned.

"I forgot that was today. Well, tell him I came by, will you?"

He sniffed the air.

"You been sucking on peppermints?"

I nodded.

"Yes sir. I've been having a breath problem. Something to do with puberty, I think. Everything's starting to stink."

He grinned broadly.

"Yeah, we've noticed Hank is starting to get a little rank around the edges. That reminds me, he said to tell you he can't go to Granger's Lake this afternoon. His mama has him helping her with the yard."

"Okay, thanks. I'll tell Daddy you came by."

He waved and walked back to his car.

I shut the door, staggered to my room and passed out.

That was a small beginning to a big problem.

I used to sneak the key whenever I got a chance. Once I figured out which bottles tasted the best mixed with Coke or 7-Up, I would pour some out into a mason jar and hide it in my room. I learned to gargle with minty mouthwash and made a habit of sucking on breath mints. My parents teased me about wanting to make a good impression on the girls, and I pretended that's what it was about.

I began to pay attention to what my father drank. I soon discovered that there were bottles in the cabinet that he almost never touched. When I tried a sip, I could see why.

But these were the ones it was easiest for me to sneak from, adding a bit of water to keep the level from dropping too fast. By this time, I wasn't in it for the flavor anyway, but for the buzz. So it didn't matter how bad it tasted. If I could sneak more of it without getting caught, that was the thing.

I never got in trouble as a teenager because of my drinking. I never got caught, although there were some close calls. It was only after I started college that I got pulled over for erratic driving. And my grades never suffered in school. I was smart and in those days was able to control my drinking somewhat, knowing enough not to get smashed the night before things like taking the SATs. Which I knocked out of the park, by the way, scoring a near perfect 1596.

I had always been susceptible to colds, and that covered a multitude of headachy mornings, red noses and bleary eyes. I was young and otherwise healthy and able to keep ahead of the wave of disaster that was inexorably rolling toward me.

I had heard about alcoholics, of course, and seen drunks on television and in movies. But those people were poor and ignorant and dirty. I was at the top of my class, from the richest family in town and showered regularly. I didn't have a problem. I just liked to have a little fun.

Hank knew I drank, of course, because I told him everything. Heck, I bragged about it. So when he was feeling rotten after that game, it wasn't too hard to get him to try it. But he had such a hangover the next day that he swore he would never do it again. His parents had been so concerned that they almost took him to the emergency room, but he convinced them he was just exhausted and that he had eaten a bad burrito grande at Tiny's.

But Hank did drink again, and that was my fault, too. And it turned out to be much worse than dealing with a hangover.

When we graduated high school, I was valedictorian and LuNella was salutatorian. For some reason, she was a nervous wreck and barely got through her speech. By the end of the ceremony, she was shaking like a leaf and threw up all over the back of Hank's car on the way to the all-night party the parents of the graduating seniors traditionally threw. Hank drove her home to get cleaned up, but once she was there, she refused to go to the party.

She was embarrassed by her performance at graduation, felt sick and just wanted to go to bed. Hank pleaded and pleaded. This was the biggest night of their lives, he said – funny how little perspective we had at that age – and everyone would wonder where she was. And what were the guys going to say if he showed up without a date? And the girls would all be gossiping about her and thinking they had broken up.

But his wheedling and threatening availed him naught. LuNella had made up her mind. She was not used to looking like a fool and she had had enough of it for one night. She kissed him goodnight and sent him away.

It was a much subdued Hank who showed up at the party half an hour later. I was there with Linda Moberly, the girl I had been dating for about six weeks. She saw Hank come in and poked me.

"Where's LuNella?" she asked.

She and LuNella were not the best of friends.

"I don't know. Hang on."

I got up and sauntered over to Hank.

"Well, a dillar, a dollar and all that. Where you been? And where's your lady?"

He told me what had happened and we went back to the table where Linda was now talking to Chanice Wackerly. Chanice was a chesty junior who should not have been at the party. But her brother Will had graduated and his parents were helping foot the bill. Chanice was supposed to be helping serve the buffet, but she had slipped out of her "Congrats, Grads!" paper apron and was mingling.

"LuNella's sick," I said to Linda as Hank and I sat down.

"Too bad," Linda said. "Hank, you're going to be all alone."

She looked at Chanice.

"Don't you think that's sad, Chanice? Hank's all alone. Maybe you can cheer him up."

Chanice moved closer to Hank and said, "Want company, big boy?"

She said it in a fake Hollywood starlet voice and we all laughed. Hank had been pouting because he was so angry at LuNella for leaving him in the lurch, but I could tell by the look on his face that he was thinking he could get back at her by doing a little harmless flirting.

I passed him a can of soda that I had doctored with the vodka I had stashed in the trunk of my car.

He took a sip without looking and then pulled back.

"What the …?"

"Just drink it, buddy," I told him. "You just graduated. Your girl is sick at home. It'll make you feel better."

He drank it and passed it to Chanice.

Four trips to my car later, Hank and Chanice disappeared. I was busy with Linda and didn't give it any thought.

Late the next afternoon, I finally woke up and drove over to Hank's house. His mother answered the door with a scowl on her face and told me he was still in bed.

"We think he got drunk last night," she confided. "Were any of those boys drinking?"

"Not that I saw," I lied cheerfully. "And you know Hank. He wouldn't drink even if everyone else there was. Kind of like not jumping off a cliff, you know."

She didn't look convinced and I went away.

That night Hank called me and we had a long talk. He and Chanice had gotten drunk, but that wasn't the big story. He had lost his virginity that night. Chanice was a bit more experienced, which was not a big surprise. We had heard the stories. He felt terrible, but

I told him not to worry about it. No big deal. Lots of kids did the dirty after prom or on graduation night. He was a grown man now. Act like it.

We thought that was the end of the matter until Chanice called Hank six weeks later to let him know she was pregnant. Naturally he hadn't used a condom. Poor guy! He was such a gentleman he hadn't planned ahead.

Chanice was calm. She wanted to get an abortion and keep the whole thing a secret. Hank wasn't sure, but I told him that was the right thing to do. LuNella had heard about him making out with Chanice and it had taken him two weeks to get her to forgive him for that. What would happen if she heard this? I said I would drive them over to Austin and we would get everything taken care of and no one would ever be the wiser. Chanice called a clinic, made an appointment and we were all set. I breathed a sigh of relief.

Too soon, as it turned out.

Because my friend Hank, that perfect gentleman, moped around and his father finally asked him what was wrong. And Hank blurted the whole story out to his Baptist deacon father.

Which put an end to our plan.

That night Hank's folks took him to the Wackerlys' house and made him tell Chanice's parents. I understand that Mr. Wackerly lunged across the room and tried to grab Hank by the throat, but Hank dodged him and hid in the kitchen while Chanice and her mother grabbed Mr. Wackerly and dragged him back to his chair. Mrs. Wackerly yelled for her son Will, who had played center on the football team and was strong as an ox. He wasn't the brightest ox on the team, but he did what he was told. She made him stand behind his father with his big farm boy hands on the old man's shoulders throughout the rest of the interview.

At the end of which time, Hank and Chanice were engaged. Hank's father used the Wackerlys' phone to call the Baptist minister and arrange for a wedding the following week. They said goodbye to the Wackerlys, no one shook hands and the Ingrams drove off under glowering skies.

My role as provider of the alcohol that proved Hank's undoing came out in the yelling and screaming of accusations. Needless to say, despite what Hank and LuNella and I had planned, I was never going to be best man at his wedding.

Hank never spoke to me again except in the most distant and formal way. He had been a gentleman for too long to treat me nastily, at least at first. But he avoided eye contact and just nodded when we passed on the street. He never answered my phone calls and his parents hung up on me when they recognized my voice. I even tried writing him a few times. The letters didn't come back, but there was never a response. I'm not sure he even got them. I wouldn't put it past his parents to be opening his mail at that point. Friends told me that they were also saying that I did drugs and had been accused of dealing.

It was true that I had been accused of dealing. But I wasn't, and the Ingrams were the ones who accused me. They never mentioned that point when they spread the tales.

LuNella was crushed. She had been blindsided by hearing about Hank and Chanice making out and the pregnancy was beyond her worst fears. She told me Hank never even called her to try to explain, but I blame his parents for that, too. Or maybe her parents. I'm sure they would have refused to let him talk to her if he had called.

What with one thing and another, LuNella had lost her enthusiasm for Texas A&M after what happened with Hank. Instead she went to Sam Houston State University in Huntsville, a prison town an hour north of where I was in Houston. She majored in elementary education and did well, but she never quite fit in with the Huntsville crowd. She did join the Tri Delts, but I think more to satisfy her mother than herself.

We talked a lot on the phone, drawing closer in our pain and loss, talking into the small hours about how much it hurt and how unfair life was. Because she was relatively nearby, I went to see her from time to time or brought her into Houston to hang out with me and my friends. Eventually hanging out turned into casual dating, which turned into more serious dating and finally, by the time we graduated from our respective universities, we got married.

I think I loved her. I know she didn't love me the way she loved Hank, but that was okay. Somehow I thought I owed her a life after what I had done. I was arrogant enough in those days to think she was lucky to get me.

If Hank had been distant before our wedding, he overcame his gentlemanly ways afterward. He became verbally hostile when we passed on the street and took to turning his head to spit when I came into view.

Things were not going well for him and Chanice. She was a nice enough girl, but her pregnancy had ended Hank's dreams in more ways than one. Not only did he lose LuNella, he lost his chance at A&M. The Baptist Aggie alumnus who sponsored Hank's scholarship withdrew it when he learned that Hank was planning to arrive on campus with a four-months pregnant wife.

So instead of the football powerhouse school he had always dreamed of, Hank went to Windham Community College in Davis for a year. Trying to support a family he didn't want while commuting an hour each way to a school he hated did not work. He dropped out after a year and went to work for Peck's Pecans. His father got him the job, and my father thought it was the least he could do for Hank, given what I had done to him. I heard about that at dinner every night for weeks.

And my father wondered why I drank!

I suspected that having to work for my family galled Hank, but there were few options in Blakesfield. He and Chanice were living in a trailer on the back of his parents' property. She had a job as a checkout girl at the Pik-n-Stik for a while, but the pregnancy got complicated and she wound up having to keep to her bed for six months.

When Hank, Junior was born, he was a healthy nine pounds, six ounces. But the pregnancy and long labor took a toll on Chanice. Her fragile pale prettiness faded away, she grew plump and then stout and then fat. I heard that she fought with Hank all the time, blaming one another for the disaster their lives had become.

I also heard that about the only thing they agreed on was that the person who bore the most blame was Corny Shane. And they spread that around town. Rumors of my drinking escapades and brushes with the law circulated as well, and people found it easy to believe I had ruined my best friend's life and stolen his girl.

Maybe because there was more than a grain of truth in it, but that hadn't been my plan.

Not that my own plans had worked out all that well.

All this ran through my mind in a flash when Katie asked, "What's he got against me?"

I hugged her and stroked her hair.

"Boys are boys, sweetie," I said sadly. "There's no accounting for what they do."

Chapter 13

The next day Miss Missouri took Katie to Bible school at the Methodist Church. She told me later that Joanne hadn't stirred anything up. Apparently she had heard that Angelo had not been at the park and thought the episode was over and done.

I had mixed feelings. I wanted to be happy that Angelo might be gone, but at the same time I resented Joanne thinking she had anything to do with it. And I hated the hurt look in Katie's eyes. Maybe she was learning that there is no accounting for what boys do even when those boys have wings.

After lunch I took Billy Bob into the living room with me and lay down on the couch for a father-son nap. This is an important part of bonding, in my opinion. Our couch is nice and comfortable, and he fell asleep lying on his stomach on my chest. I felt like I was in one of those old Kodak moment ads.

Belinda came by just as Billy Bob and I were getting settled. She and Katie were going to the park, and they went out the front door giggling.

I dozed off and on for almost an hour. Thing came in and began to complain that she was hungry. I ignored her as long as I could, but she finally got up on the couch and played the trump card. She didn't poke me, she poked at Billy Bob. That got him wriggling and there was nothing left to do but get up and feed the cat.

Thing is Katie's cat. I'm not anti-feline but neither am I a big fan. When Miss Missouri wanted to give my daughter the calico kitten with the blank face three year before, I was reluctant. But LuNella had thought it would help teach Katie responsibility if we insisted that she had to feed the cat and clean its litter box.

And I had to say, Katie had been very faithful in fulfilling her duties. She kept Thing's food dish and her water dish clean and full all the time. She also gave the cat teeth-cleaning treats. The vet had recommended that she give Thing a few in the morning and a few in the evening. Somehow that had morphed into a few in the morning, one at noon, one at one, one at two and so on. The cat's food dish was always full, but she came around almost on the hour demanding the treat. When Katie wasn't around, I was the target of the demands.

I sat up carefully and lay Billy Bob on the couch between a couple of small cushions to make sure he didn't roll himself off onto the floor. The treats were in a glass container by the television and Thing was walking in circles under it, flicking her tail and making her special "Treat me, treat me" noise. I got one of the green fish-shaped bits out and dropped it in front of her. She dived on it.

"No 'Thank you?'" I said, putting the top back on the container.

She looked up, not to respond but no doubt hoping I would give her another one. She made the noise, but I wasn't having any. She sat down, lifted a hind leg and began to groom herself.

Billy Bob was acting like he wanted a treat, too. I picked him up, checked to make sure he didn't need changing and, reassured as to his dry state, went into the kitchen.

"Here you go, buddy boy," I said, maneuvering squirming legs into place in his high chair and getting a bib onto him.

"Ka-ka!" he said with a toothy grin.

"Let's not go there, okay?" I said, shaking my head at him.

He babbled with delight.

I found a small jar of applesauce and opened it. Ten minutes later, I had managed to get almost as much inside Billy Bob as he had managed to get on me. All in all, not too bad. I wiped his face and made a mental note to tuck a dish towel under my chin next time. I wonder if someone makes matching child-parent bib sets? I'd have to look online.

I started a cup of coffee brewing and took Billy Bob back to his crib. When I got there, I discovered his status was no longer dry, and taking care of that situation took a while. He thinks it is great fun to get cleaned up and likes to drag it out as long as possible. It was not my favorite job, but I managed. I got him settled in the crib, turned the mobile on and waited until he was semi-hypnotized by its motion before I headed back for my coffee.

I had just finished and was rinsing my cup when I heard the back door creak and Katie came in.

"Hey!" she said.

I put the mug into the dishwasher and dried my hands.

"Well, you're in a better mood. Did y'all have fun at the park?"

"Yes, sir," she said. "And Angelo was back."

No wonder she was pleased. I couldn't hold back a grin. So much for Joanne's hopes, I thought.

"Yes," she said happily. "He was already there when we got there."

"And what did y'all do?"

She sat down and picked at a spot on the table.

"You know. Stuff. Ran around. Played on the swings. Talked."

"Who talked?"

She looked up.

"Okay, I talked. He listened. He's such a good listener."

I laughed.

"You think he's a good listener because he can't talk back. Don't expect every boy to be that cooperative."

A sudden thought occurred to me.

"Do you think Angelo can talk but maybe he can't speak English?"

She shook her head.

"I don't think so. I mean, when I talk to him or when Belinda does or one of the other kids, he acts like he understands. If we tell him how to play a game, for instance, he always knows what we mean."

"Well, you know, when I was working at the orchards, we had a lot of Mexicans out there who didn't speak English, or not much, but who understood a lot of what we said."

She nodded.

"Yeah, like Ana Luisa at school. She's one of the cafeteria ladies and she's very nice. I don't think she knows how to say much but when I tell her what I want, she understands."

"Right, like that."

"But I don't think it's the same. I noticed that when I tell Ana Luisa something and she doesn't understand it right, she smiles and nods anyway. But she gets it wrong. She gives me potatoes when I wanted rice. But Angelo isn't like that. He doesn't make mistakes."

"But he never talks?"

She shook her head.

"He never makes any sound at all."

Thing walked in and began making feline demands. Katie picked her up and held her in her lap and the cat turned on the purr machine.

"He's not like Sweet Thing. He doesn't make noises that aren't English words. He just doesn't make any noise."

She stopped and tilted her head for a moment, lost in thought. She stopped stroking Thing and the cat bumped her hand with her head until she started up again.

"Even when he's running around, he doesn't make any sounds. You know how you yell and laugh and stuff. He doesn't do that. The only sound is the sound his wings make. And even they don't always make noise, not when he's just moving them real slow and sort of hanging in the air. He does that a lot, hangs in the air."

She looked down at Thing and pulled the cat to her chest. Thing doesn't like to be held tight. She struggled and hopped down. Twitch, twitch of the tail and a stately exit.

Katie looked up.

"I wonder what it would be like to fly," she said. "It would be so cool. Don't you think?"

"I certainly do," I admitted, "but I guess we will never know. Maybe someday when you are older, though, we can go hang gliding. That's probably the closest we will ever get."

"Could we? Really? For my birthday maybe?"

"Okay, but maybe not this next birthday. Maybe for a special one, like when you are sixteen. Or eighteen. Or twenty-one. Twenty-one sounds good to me."

She frowned.

"That's forever off! I bet if I was a boy, you'd take me when I was twelve."

She stormed out. She was probably right. I was still not sure what a little girl could do and not get broken.

That night at dinner I tried to make peace over meatloaf and sweet potato fries.

"Did you ask Angelo to come to Bible school?" I asked.

I wasn't only being conciliatory. I was interested in what would happen.

"I did. I explained what it was and how we sang songs and heard stories about Jesus and made stuff. I'm not sure he understood all that," she admitted. "I mean I think he understood the words but maybe not what it was all about."

"Do you think he'll come?"

"I don't know. I asked him but he didn't nod yes or anything. On the other hand, he didn't shake his head no. He does that, you know. He can nod his head yes or shake it no."

"So he doesn't talk," I pointed out, "but he does use a sort of sign language."

"A little bit, I guess," she said.

Wednesday Miss Missouri gave Katie a ride to Holiness Tabernacle for Bible school. I spent the morning with Billy Bob, trying to get him to say more words, giving him juice in the sippy cup that he had been learning to use and generally bonding. When he started yawning, I put him in the crib and sat in the rocker in the corner, reading the Big Book.

I heard Miss Missouri's car pulling into her drive before I realized it was lunch time, and I hadn't done anything yet. I hopped up, checked on Billy Bob dozing and headed to the kitchen, tossing the book onto my bed as I passed my bedroom.

When Katie came in the back door, I was putting together some tuna salad. It was easy and Katie loved it in a sandwich or on top of a bowl of lettuce and other veggies. Not a Wayne meal.

I was not a big tuna fan when I was a kid. My mother's youngest sister used to joke about babysitting Richard and me when I was three and Richard was still a baby. I asked her what we were having for lunch and she told me she was making tuna fish.

"Now, Molly." I said sternly, "you know tuna fish won't hold me up!"

At some point I learned to like tuna, but most of my family still thought that I didn't care for it. At least I assumed they thought that. They didn't talk to me about what I liked or didn't like. Or anything else.

"Do you want a sandwich or salad?" I asked Katie when she came back from putting her Bible away.

"Sandwich, please," she said, sitting down.

I reached up to the top of the refrigerator and pulled down a plastic bag filled with whole wheat pita.

My father liked white bread and white bread only. My mother tried every trick in the book to get him to eat something else, but he refused. I liked to think the fact that I couldn't stand the stuff had nothing to do with stubborn rebellion on my part. But whatever the case, I didn't care for it. Katie had been raised on wheat bread and as far as I knew, she was happy with it.

"All I have is pita, okay?"

"That's fine."

I broke a pita in half, opened the pockets and stuffed them with the tuna.

"Pickle?" I asked, getting the jar of homemade dill pickles from the refrigerator.

"No, just the sandwich."

I put her sandwich on a plate, added a handful of shoestring potatoes and handed it to her. I did the same for myself and put half a dill pickle on the side.

"Well?" I said,

She swallowed a bite of sandwich and picked up some shoestring potatoes.

"Well, what?" she grinned.

"Did he show up?"

"He did."

She put the potatoes in her mouth and chewed.

"And …?"

"And nothing, I guess. He was standing outside the church when Miss Missouri and I got there. Belinda was talking to him and when she saw me, she waved and they came over. We took him into church with us. I wanted to sit in the back, but Belinda said we had to sit up front. But I told her that if we did that, Angelo's wings would stick up too high and the kids behind us wouldn't be able to see. Finally we found him a seat on the end of a row where no one was behind him and that worked out."

"And no one got upset?"

She shook her head, but then said, "Well, Miss Smithers didn't look happy when she saw us. But Angelo just sat there and didn't make any noise, so I guess she thought it was okay. I saw her talking to some of the other preachers, but nobody did anything. Miss Missouri sat with us and I think that helped."

I was sure it did. Miss Missouri had probably been the fifth grade teacher for every preacher in the place. If the boy with the wings was under her protection in some way, they weren't going to mess with him. Not while she was there to see it, anyway.

Katie took another bite of her sandwich and picked at the shoestring potatoes.

"Then he went with us to Miss Missouri's class. He listened to the story but I don't think he was interested. He kept looking around the room and the pictures on the wall. He kept pointing at one of a bunch of angels and grinning. Miss Missouri finally told him to settle down, and he did. When class was over and we went for our snack, though, he went outside and didn't come back."

I could hear the disappointment in her voice.

"Well, Katie, maybe he didn't understand it all. Or maybe he was bored. Boys get bored pretty easily, you know."

I imagined if I were a boy with wings, I could think of lots of things I would rather do on a summer morning instead of sitting in a

Sunday school room listening to stories and looking at cartoonish angel pictures. I was surprised he had shown up in the first place.

"I guess," she said. "Miss Missouri said the same thing."

"Well, she should know, teaching all those years," I said, getting up and wiping crumbs off my plate and into the trash can under the sink. "Do you think he'll be at the park?"

"I don't know. But Belinda asked if I could go with her and Toby to the mall this afternoon in Davis. Her mama is taking them over to get some school clothes."

I took her empty plate, wiped it clean and put it in the sink with mine.

"I guess it's okay. When does school start? I guess I need to take you over there myself and get some clothes pretty soon."

"Two weeks to school. I don't want to buy anything yet. I want to just look around and see what they have. Maybe we could go to Austin?"

Austin was 200 miles away, a three hour drive each way.

"Well, I'll think about it. That's a long way to go for a couple of pairs of jeans and some tee shirts."

She looked indignant.

"Daddy, I want more than a couple of pairs of plain old jeans and some tee shirts. I'm going to be in middle school. I need some nice clothes!"

"Gotta look good for the boys, huh?" I teased. "Do you have your eye on anyone in particular? Do I need to take someone aside and warn him how to treat my daughter?"

She looked horrified and then saw that I was joking.

"I'm not thinking of anyone special," she said. "Middle school boys are so immature."

She said *immature* with that special feminine intonation that implied that all boys were children and not to be taken seriously. I wondered if that included boys with wings.

"I think you said Angelo is the age of a middle school boy, didn't you? Is he immature?"

"Angelo," she said, turning pink, "isn't like the others. Thank goodness!"

She turned on her heel and walked out of the kitchen.

I cleaned up the kitchen and went to get Billy Bob and feed him. By the time he was ready to lie down again, Margaret Scranton and her children were at the front door for Katie.

"Now, Corny, do you want me to get some things for Katie while we're in Davis? I'm just putting everything on my credit card anyway and you could pay me back."

Like I said, a very nice lady.

Before I could answer, though, Katie broke in and said, "Daddy said he may take me to Austin to look for school clothes."

Margaret looked at me with surprise. She knew I couldn't drive to Blakesfield, much less to Austin.

"I told her I would think about it. Katie, you know we can't do that by ourselves. We'd have to get someone to take us and that would be an imposition. So why don't you see if there's anything you want in Davis and if Mrs. Scranton is willing to go ahead and get it …"

Katie seldom showed her temper, but her face hardened.

"I want to go to Austin! I bet Miss Missouri would take us. Or Wayne. Or someone. Please! Please!"

I looked at Margaret and said, "Why don't you just let Katie look around today and see if she finds anything she might want. I'll find a way to take her shopping later, but" I turned to Katie, "we may have to go to Davis. Austin is a long way off."

Katie nodded.

"But you'll think about it?"

"I'll think about it."

As they turned to go, Margaret held back and said in a low voice, "When my daddy used to tell me he'd think about it, that was just a nice way of saying no."

I nodded.

"A lot of us daddies go to the same school."

She laughed and headed to car.

I was looking in the freezer wondering what to make for dinner when the phone rang. It was Margaret calling to say that they had been delayed in Davis. A tractor trailer hauling cases of honey had overturned right at the entrance and exit to Wally World and the road was covered with golden stickiness. The police, such as they were in Davis, were trying to direct traffic around the mess and it looked like it would be a while before Margaret and the kids would get through. She suggested that Katie eat dinner with them and, if they got back to Blakesfield in time, they would take her to Wednesday night Bible service and then bring her home.

A tractor trailer-load of honey on the road sounded like one of those things I could not change, and I thanked Margaret for taking care of everything.

"Tell the girls to bee sweet, now, ya'hear?" I joked.

She had the grace to laugh but it was clearly not an amusing situation for her, stranded in Davis on a hot August afternoon with a carload a kids asking when they were going to get to go home.

I hung up the phone and relaxed. No rush on dinner now. Billy Bob would get something out of his jars and I would eat what was left of the ham salad Ada had made. Instead of making a sandwich, though, I got out the corn chips and used the ham salad as a dip. It was mighty tasty, and I tried again not to think about the salt I was absorbing.

I was sitting on the couch with Billy Bob leaning up against me when Margaret's car pulled up in the drive about 8:30 and I heard Katie yell goodbye. Before I could get up and go to the door to thank Margaret, the headlights of the car swept across the front window as she was backing out. Katie came in laughing.

"Well, that was exciting," she said, flopping down on the sofa next to her little brother. He opened his eyes for a moment and then closed them again.

"So tell me," I said, putting down the Big Book that I had been reading.

She gave me a detailed account of the truck and the honey and said that Margaret had taken them all back into Wally World to get sandwiches at the sub shop inside. They ate and waited for the traffic snarl to work itself out. Davis, of course, is not that big a place and the mess had been cleaned up enough for them to escape when they finished their supper. Margaret had to drive carefully up over a makeshift ramp onto the median, but they made it out alive. The truck was still on its side and people were standing around scratching their heads and saying they had never seen anything like it in all their born days. Not in all their born days.

When she finally ran down, I asked about the clothes.

"Oh, Belinda got a bunch of stuff, but I didn't like anything. Everything was all glitter and fake jewels. I looked at some magazines, and they said the look now is supposed to be more like what they wore in the 60s.

I laughed.

"The 60s? You mean you want to dress the way your grandmother dressed when she was your age?"

"Daddy! Don't be ridiculous. It will be totally different. Just sort of … inspired, I think the article said."

She hopped up and headed for her bedroom.

"Anyway, not at all what they had at Wally World. We'll have to see about Austin."

I sighed. Miss Missouri was right. Katie was growing up and I wasn't ready for it by a long shot.

I picked up the Big Book but couldn't get back into it. I turned off the light and went to bed and slept well.

As it turned out, that was the last peaceful night of sleep I had for a while.

Chapter 14

The next morning was Thursday and it started quietly enough. Billy Bob ate his cereal and did not throw any of it on the floor or on me. Katie ate hers and re-read the cereal box she had studied the day before. I had my usual breakfast sandwich and wondered if I might be getting into a rut.

"Where's Vacation Bible School today?" I asked Katie as we were cleaning up in the kitchen after breakfast.

"Evangel Temple," she muttered.

I closed the dishwasher and started getting the garbage ready to take out.

"Does that worry you?"

She thought for a moment.

"Not really, I guess. I mean, Miss Smithers won't make a big fuss in her own church, will she?"

I tied the white plastic bag tight and pulled an empty one out of the box under the sink. I flapped it open and put it into the garbage can, wondering what Joanne might do if she thought Angelo's presence was a violation of her turf.

"Well," I said as I picked up the trash, "we can always hope she won't. But maybe Angelo won't be there today."

Katie nodded. Mixed emotions played across her face. If Angelo didn't show up, Joanne would have no reason to make trouble. But if Angelo didn't show up, Katie was going to be disappointed. It seemed like a lose-lose situation to me.

"Can I invite Belinda home for lunch?" she asked.

Maybe she was looking for a consolation prize in case the kid with the wings let her down. I told her that would be fine.

While Katie and Miss Missouri were at Vacation Bible School, Billy Bob and I took a stroll along Southwood Drive toward Peck's Park. We sat in the shade of the pavilion and he gurgled and dozed while I read the Big Book.

I was still trying to wrap my head around Step Two. Wayne told me I was making something complicated out of something very simple.

"Try this," he had told me on the phone the night before in exasperation. "What in your life is unmanageable at the moment?"

"The kid with the wings," I said promptly.

He sighed heavily.

"Okay, what's the real problem there?"

"I just can't stop thinking about it."

He nodded.

"You can't. Have you seriously tried to stop?"

I thought for a moment and shook my head.

"That's what I thought," Wayne said. "So for the next, let's say twelve hours, every time you catch yourself thinking about it, I want you to just stop."

"Just stop?"

"Just stop. Try anything you want to that will make you stop, but just stop. Now what time is it?"

I looked at my watch.

"Ten fifteen."

"Tomorrow morning at ten fifteen, I want you to call me and tell me how that goes."

At ten o'clock, I checked on Billy Bob. He had dozed off in his stroller. I walked a little distance away where I could keep an eye on him and still talk on the phone without waking him up.

"What's the story?" Wayne said as soon as he answered his phone. "Did you stop thinking about the guy with wings?"

I gave a snort.

"I did not. I tried, I really did. But all that happened was I gave myself a splitting headache with all the effort and still kept finding my mind wandering right back to Angelo."

I could imagine Wayne nodding.

"That's what I thought would happen. Now I want you to try something different. Next time you think of this kid, instead of trying to stop, just say to the universe at large, 'Please take this thought away and give me serenity.' That's all. Ever time you think of Angelo and his wings, ask the universe to take the thought away and give you serenity."

"And what's that supposed to do?"

"I can't tell you what it is supposed to do. I just want you to do it and call me tonight about ten fifteen."

"Okay, I'll try it," I said, doubt oozing from every pore. "But you know Katie will talk about him and who knows who else. How am I going to stop thinking about him when people are talking about him all around me?"

"What I want you to do," Wayne said, "is to try to turn it over when you find yourself all on your own thinking about him. People talking about him and engaging you in conversation about him, that stuff all falls into the things-I-cannot-change category. You pay attention to when you start thinking about him when you are on your own. That's all."

I shook my head and noticed that Billy Bob was starting to wake up. I headed back toward him and said goodbye to Wayne, promising to try his exercise.

"That's all I'm asking," he said. "Like most things, it's just a suggestion. We'll try it and see if it works. If it does, fine. If not, then we chalk that up to experience and we try something else.

People in this program learn to quit drinking, but they also learn not to be quitters."

Yeah, yeah, I thought, clicking off the phone. More bumper sticker philosophy.

But I gave it a shot the first time I thought of Angelo while I was pushing Billy Bob's stroller back to the house.

"Hello, universe, it's me, Corny," I said sarcastically. "I know, you being the universe and all that my little problem must seem minuscule to you, but it is driving me up the wall. So if you don't mind, please take this thought away from me and grant me serenity."

I walked on a few steps, thinking perhaps my attitude was lousy. I tried again.

"I'm sorry if that sounded rude, but, hey! You're the universe and you're big enough to handle it, right?"

Still sounding smart ass, Corny Shane, I told myself. *Try again*. I remembered the theme song of an old situation comedy about some young doctors. It had a line in it something like, *I can't do this on my own; I'm no superman.*

Maybe I needed to stop trying to be superman. I took a deep breath.

"I can't do this on my own. Please take this thought away and give me serenity." I paused and added softly, "Amen."

I don't know if the universe heard me or if it was just that Billy Bob chose that moment to start wiggling around, but I forgot about Angelo for the rest of the way home. I was too busy trying to keep my son entertained. He twisted his mouth around in a way that I had come to recognize as a call for changing. I babbled to him, hoping to distract him enough to prevent an outpouring of wails and tears, and picked up my pace. We made it to the house without any weeping, on Billy Bob's part or mine, but once I started getting him out of the stroller, he let loose. Thing was sitting on the couch and looked at us with disdain, curled up and put her tail over her ears.

After cleaning Billy Bob's bottom and getting him into clean training pants, I put him in his crib. He said "Papa" a few times during the process. I rewarded him each time with a huge smile and a kiss. Positive reinforcement, right? Of course, he lifted his arms up and waved them. I assume he wanted to be held, but maybe he wanted the mobile turned on. I switched it on and he settled down. I gave him another kiss and headed to the kitchen. It was getting close to lunchtime and Katie should be back soon, and I needed to have something for her and her guest. Or guests? Maybe Angelo would be with her, too.

I decided to take advantage of Belinda's visit to clean out some of the leftovers. I put out small bowls of tuna salad and a plate of pita bread, cut a few slices of pizza up into smaller pieces and zapped them in the microwave, sliced a tomato and put it on a serving dish alongside lettuce leaves, dill pickle spears and carrot sticks. There were a few radishes in the crisper drawer, looking like they were fast approaching their expiration date. I washed them up and cut them into rosettes. Even if the girls didn't eat them, they made the veggie plate look fancy.

I stood back to look at what I had wrought and was congratulating myself when I heard the back door open and two giggling girls ran in.

"Daddy! You won't believe what happened," Katie said, flopping down into her usual chair.

Belinda, whose mother raised her children properly, said, "Hello, Mr. Shane. Thank you for inviting me to lunch."

I smiled at the little redhead,

"You're always welcome, Belinda. Have a seat and fill your plates. Then you can tell me what I won't believe."

Youthful hunger won out over youthful eagerness to tell a story and the next few minutes were taken up with the girls politely offering one another what each one considered either the choicest morsel or the things each didn't want. In Belinda's case, I think it was the former motive. In Katie's, I'm not so sure. She's a good kid, but she has a streak of rationalization that she inherited from me.

Of me it is truly said that I always have two reasons for the things I do: A good reason and the real reason. On occasion they even coincide.

The girls finally got themselves served while I poured them glasses of sweet tea. I sat down and filled my own plate. I stuffed tuna, tomato and lettuce into a pita pocket and was putting it into my mouth when I notice the girls were looking at me expectantly.

I put the sandwich down.

"Do I have something on my face?" I asked.

Katie shook her head.

"Belinda's family says a prayer before eating," she explained.

"Okay," I turned to our guest, "do you want to say the blessing for us, Belinda?"

She turned pink.

"Oh, no sir! That's a job for the man. It says so in the Bible."

Really? I thought.

"Okay, then I guess it's up to me."

I searched my memory and came up with the prayer my own family used to say perfunctorily before every meal.

"Bless us, O Lord, and these thy gifts which we are about to receive from thy bounty. Amen."

The girls chorused, "Amen."

Belinda picked up a pickle spear, but before she bit into it, she whispered to me, "You're supposed to say 'In Jesus's name' but I guess it's okay, you being Catholic and all."

"Thank you, Belinda," I said.

Oh, Jesus! I wondered what she would have said if I had prayed in the name of the universe.

"Now girls, what am I not going to believe?" I said, biting into my sandwich and changing the subject.

Either one of them could have told me the whole story in a third of the time that it took both of them. There was a great deal of backtracking and disagreement over unimportant details, and they constantly interrupted one another. It kept them busy and me entertained long past the time we were actually eating. They were so involved that they consumed everything I had put on the table, including, to my amazement, the radish roses.

What the story boiled down to was this.

When everyone arrived at Evangel Temple that morning, Joanne Smithers was waiting on the front steps. That was not unusual, it being her day to host things. But she was scanning the arrivals and periodically peering up into the sky, clearly on the lookout for anyone with wings, whether on land or in the air. When time came for the opening service to begin, no winged beings – none visible to the crowd, at any rate – had appeared and Joanne went inside.

After a couple of announcements and an opening prayer, she led the teachers and student in a song:

The one way to peace is the power of the cross.
His banner over me is love!
The one way to peace is the power of the cross.
His banner over me is love!
The one way to peace is the power of the cross.

His banner over me is love!
His banner over me is love!

It is not a song I knew, but the girls gave me a wobbly rendition so I would get the sense. Apparently just as they were getting to the final *His banner over me is love!*, the double doors to the sanctuary opened up and Angelo flew in, holding a big bouquet of flowers. He circled the sanctuary and stopped in front of Joanne, whose voice had faded out and left her mouth hanging open. Angelo gently touched down, handed her the flowers and grinned. Then he calmly turned around and went to find a seat between Katie and Miss Missouri.

For a moment, not a sound was heard.

Then, as Belinda put it, Joanne had a hissy fit. She screamed and threw the flowers down like they burned her hands. She looked around the room in a panic and ran out of the sanctuary.

Chaos erupted. Half of the adults jumped up and ran after Joanne. The other half struggled to calm the kids. Once order was shakily restored, Miss Missouri led them in several songs, and then announced that they would have their snacks before going to class. The other teachers who had remained led their students out of the sanctuary to the cafeteria. Angelo trooped out with Katie and Belinda. Miss Missouri disappeared through the door Joanne had taken on her flight from the sanctuary.

After the kids had eaten their cookies and drunk their punch, they followed signs to assigned classrooms. Miss Missouri was waiting for her class and immediately started in on the material. Belinda and Katie sat on either side of Angelo like guards, and everyone else shied away. Miss Missouri explained that Miss Smithers must have seen a bee in the flower bouquet and it frightened her. Fortunately she had not been stung and was all right.

She made a point of thanking everyone, including Angelo, for being so grown-up and remaining calm. It did not sound like many of them had stayed calm, but I figured Miss Missouri was appealing to their pride and hoping that they might want to remember thing the way she was telling it.

"Was there a bee?" I asked.

Katie and Belinda looked at one another and shrugged.

"Who knows? None of us saw it. But there were a lot of red wasps around the church when we got there."

I let it pass.

Chapter 15

The girls helped me clean up and then asked if they could play with Billy Bob. I suggested that they bring him to the kitchen and feed him for me, and they agreed. I made sure they had him safely secured in his high chair and left them to it while I went next door to consult with Miss Missouri.

Her version of what had happened at Evangel Temple was similar to what the girls had told me, with one notable exception.

"I told the kids that Joanne was frightened by a bee. Actually she claimed that the flowers were covered with wasps and that Angelo had known it when he handed them to her. She says it was a direct attack."

I frowned.

"Did she explain how he flew through the church with a wasp-covered bouquet without loosing a swarm on everyone?"

Miss Missouri snorted.

"Explaining is not Joanne's long suit, Corny, you should know that. Like so many of her kind, she asserts rather than explains. Fred Phillips asked her the same thing, but she just became hysterical and said everyone was afraid of the boy and that's why they wouldn't do anything. It was obvious, she said, that he knew she had seen him for what he is and that was why he attacked her. Fred and Langton Hughes managed to quieten her down by the time I left to teach my class. But I don't think this is over, Corny. When I was leaving, I overheard her talking about getting a petition to ban Angelo from town."

"Ban him? How do you ban a kid who can fly?"

She looked at me seriously.

"Corny, this is the great State of Texas. You think nobody's gonna take a pot shot at the kid if Joanne stirs things up?"

"Hell and damnation!" I said and went back to check on Billy Bob and his babysitters.

The girls had fed Billy Bob and washed his face. When I came in they were trying to get him to say Katie. They helped me get him settled for his nap and then headed out to the park for the afternoon. I got my Big Book and sat down to read.

The phone rang in the middle of the afternoon. It was Miss Missouri telling me that Joanne had indeed run around town with a petition and that a town meeting had been called that night to discuss what to do. I cursed and hung up.

I was thinking about calling Wayne when it struck me that, for all the conversations and drama about Angelo, I had not been thinking about him on my own. Not obsessing about him, at any rate.

Hmm. Maybe the universe or Someone or something was looking out for me after all.

Blakesfield's town hall was an old yellow brick building that had been a one-room schoolhouse. It contained a cramped office where the town clerk and her assistant, who also handled the town treasurer duties, worked amid piles of papers stacked several feet high around their desks. Extension cords and computer cables stretched over and around the paperwork. It had to be in violation of every fire code in the world, but no one ever reported it.

Beverly Shawn had been town clerk for twenty-two years, inheriting the position from her mother. She had her own filing system, if you could call it that, and was always able to lay her hands on exactly the form or document anyone came in to find. I suspected one reason she did things her way was that it provided a certain level of job security. If they tried to get rid of her, no one else would ever be able to figure out what had been going on all those years. What we would do when she died, no one knew. Probably she would hand the office over to her own daughter, the way her mother had handed it to her, along with the secrets to the paper piles.

In addition to the office, two bathrooms and a couple of storage areas – including what had been a basement tornado shelter that had been converted into a cache for old files – the hall had a tiny auditorium with a stage at one end. Usually a row of rectangular folding tables ran the length of the room, and the council met there.

When there was a meeting like the one called that night, two tables were set up on the stage so that the council members could sit there looking official. A square speaker sat under the table, attached by a long cord to a microphone that stood in front of the town manager's chair and that he could pass to other council members as needed.

The other tables were put away and folding chairs filled the space before the stage. There were about a hundred by my estimate. For regular town meetings, ten chairs would have been ample. But Joanne had stirred up her troops. The chairs were filled and people stood along the walls on each side and in the back. There was a twangy murmur when I walked in and looked around for a seat.

I had arranged with Russelene Watts to babysit Katie and Billy Bob. Katie was getting to the age where she thought she should be able to do without a baby sitter. She pointed out that Belinda baby sat for some of her neighbors already. I trusted Katie and knew she was responsible. But I didn't want to leave her alone in the house at night with Billy Bob. If something happened, I figured it was better to have at least a teenager on site.

Russelene Watts was a freckle-faced high school junior and some relation to Miss Missouri. She had an older brother named

Russel. His parents made the mistake of telling Russel that he could name his baby sister, and he chose Russelene.

"Don't you mean Rosalynn?" his mother asked.

"No. Russelene."

And Russelene it stayed.

Despite her unusual name, Russelene was an intelligent and practical young woman, and she had been babysitting since she was twelve. Even as I wrote that, I realized that Katie was almost twelve. Oh, rats!

After a minute, I gave up and made my way along the line of men holding up the back wall and found a place to wedge myself between a couple of people I didn't recognize. That was unusual. I had grown up in Blakesfield and pretty much lived here my whole life. I thought I knew everybody. Maybe these were members of Joanne's church who drove over from a nearby town or from out in the country somewhere.

The five council members were talking among themselves at the front of the room, shuffling around a handful of papers and glancing up at the old school clock on the back wall occasionally. A few minutes after seven, they settled back and Rob Dankins cleared his throat and looked out at the crowd, waiting for silence. Waiting didn't work and he resorted to banging the gavel on the table. When that didn't produce the desired result, Beverly leaned over and turned the knob on the speaker until feedback made everyone stick their fingers in their ears and things quieted down.

"Okay, folks, let's begin," Dankins said. "We're here – "

"Hey!" someone shouted from the back, "Ain't we gotta say the Pledge of Allegiance?"

Dankins frowned, whispered to Beverly who sat beside him taking notes, and rose to his feet.

"Please rise for the Pledge of Allegiance. And you men, take off those damn caps."

People rustled to their feet, baseball caps and stained cowboy hats came off and people turned to face the flag at the side of the stage, placing hands over hearts and mumbling, "I pledge …"

When it was over, Dankins glowered and said, "Okay, everyone sit down and let's get – "

"Hey! What about the prayer?" another voice called out.

Dankins rose again and looked around.

"Is Fr. Hickey here? Fr. Hickey, would you lead us in prayer?"

A rippled of disapproval ran over a number of faces in the crowd. Joanne's troops probably expected her to say the prayer. Some of the other Protestants didn't think women should lead prayer. Most of them, though, probably feared that a Catholic prayer might not serve as well as a good Protestant invocation, even one by a woman, I guess. The kind of Protestant prayers people were used to at Blakesfield public occasions like football games ran to the "Jesus, we just want to …" variety.

People got back up, some snickering and others shooting frowns at the snickerers. Hats and caps were removed again and I saw one or two people put the palm of their right hand over their left breast for a moment before realizing that this was a prayer. A few people steepled their fingers and most bowed their heads.

I half expected Fr. Hickey to begin with a sonorous, "*In nomine Patris, et Fillii* ..." but he had judged this congregation better than that. He did make a sign of the cross, but his prayer was generic and would have been appropriate to any occasion. I thought it sounded a lot like the blessing before meals that I had learned in CCD and had recited for Belinda and Katie's benefit before lunch, but I wouldn't swear to that. He did pray "In Jesus's name," however.

"Amen!" he ended loudly and a handful of "Amens" echoed around the room.

Before sitting back down, Dankins looked around the room and demanded, "Is there anything else anyone wants me to do before we get down to business? We're going to be here all night at this rate and I, for one, want to get home to watch *CSI: San Antonio.*"

No one suggested further preliminaries and Dankins waved everyone to sit. Those who could, that is. The rest of us shifted on our feet and leaned back against the wall.

Dankins explained that the meeting had been called at the request of a group of citizens who had presented a petition to the council.

"I will ask the town clerk, Beverly Shawn, to read the letter that accompanied the petition."

Joanne had signed the letter and I assume she had written it. It went on and on for four pages, single-spaced I am sure and probably with words underline or italicized or in bold caps for emphasis. I guessed that because Beverly read it with a certain dramatic flair, whether in an attempt to communicate the letter as written or in a subtle effort to make it sound even more absurd than it was on its own. She kept a straight face throughout, but I more than half suspected she was making fun. The town clerk puts up with a lot and I am sure that Beverly would have preferred to be sitting at home in the comfort of an overstuffed chair, eating fried chicken and watching *The Bold and the Brassy* through a screen of static and television snow.

The letter was long but the gist was simple: There was a stranger in our midst and something needed to be done about it. No one knew where he came from, what he wanted or what he might be up to. He was spending time with children of the community and that was suspicious. He refused to answer questions and he was to all intents and purposes an unaccompanied minor. He was suspected of an attack on a member of the clergy. At the very least, he should be apprehended and turned over to social services, for his own protection as well as that of the town's young people.

When Beverly finished reading, there was a small spattering of claps and a few fervent "Amens" from the crowd.

"There are …" Beverly looked down, "fifteen signatures on the petition. Do you want me to read those?"

"No, that's okay," Dankins said hurriedly.

Beverly nodded but said, "I might mention that Mickey Mouse and Donald Duck appear to support this request."

That got a big laugh and I looked over at Joanne, seated in the front row. She turned a bright red and her lips tightened. I made a note to ask Miss Missouri later if there was some history between Joanne and Beverly.

Rob Dankins banged the gavel again and the laughter faded.

"Now, since you seem to be the leader of this group, Miss Smithers," he looked at her pointedly, "do you have anything to add?"

"Thank you, Your Honor," she said, which produced another wave of mirth in the crowd.

She stepped to the end of the stage and started up the steps.

Dankins stopped her.

"I think we can all hear you from where you are, Miss Smithers."

"I'll say," Beverly said in a stage whisper that they probably heard in Cherokee Creek.

Joanne glared and turned to face the crowd.

She talked for five minutes and I admit I was fascinated. Not by what she said, because that was just a rehash of what Beverly had just read to us sprinkled with unfamiliar biblical references and veiled hints about the end of times. What fascinated me was that Joanne did the whole thing without pausing to take a breath.

I leaned toward the man to my right and said, “How do you suppose she does that?”

He raised his eyebrows and grinned, “It’s really something, ain’t it? You should hear her of a Sunday morning when she really gets going.”

“Thanks,” I said out of the corner of my mouth. “I think I’ll pass.”

He nodded and murmured, “Your loss. It’s better than that *CSI* crap, that’s for sure.”

While I was thus engaged, Joanne had resumed her seat and Dankins called for further comment.

Hands shot up all over the room.

“Okay, let’s get Beverly here to write down names and then people can put their hands down so we can see who still wants to talk.”

Beverly started writing, signaling to people that she had them on the list.

While she was doing that, Dankins pleaded, “Now folks, let me ask you to do us all a favor. If someone says what you planned to say, don’t just repeat it. Things will go faster if you just say, ‘I agree with Vern’ and then sit down. Okay?”

People nodded their agreement, although I could tell that the town manager no more expected them to follow directions than I did. Which is say, we didn’t expect them to follow directions. And I guess I mean I don’t follow directions all that well either. Just ask Wayne.

The meeting lasted two and a half hours. The supporters of the petition spoke loudly and at length, but none of them was able to offer any verifiable reason that the boy was a threat. No one had been hurt, not even Joanne, no one had seen the alleged wasp except Joanne, no one had been verbally abused, none of the kids in town were the least bit afraid of him. In fact, not a single parent present reported hearing that the supposedly endangered young people were afraid.

"My kids and their friends don't pay that much attention," Dawnette Trent reported. "He's just a kid with wings. So what?"

Joanne leapt to her feet from time to time and tried in interject, but Rob Dankins hit the gavel and told her that the rules were that she couldn't talk again until everyone who wanted to talk had a chance. Joanne and her supporters were not happy, but they were, if not a minority, at least not numerous enough to force their will on the council.

I smiled. I admit I have little respect for town manager Dankins, but I admired him that night. I don't imagine he was a big fan of the boy with wings. He never struck me as a man with much imagination. The fact that he thinks *CSI: San Antonio* is high entertainment proves that. But for whatever reason, whether because he wanted to maintain his dignity as town manager or at the urging of Beverly, his town clerk, he kept things in hand.

Very few people felt compelled to say they agreed with Vern and plenty felt it necessary to repeat everything the non-existent Vern had said and then put in their own two cents' worth. Needless to say, Dankins missed *CSI.*

I had intended to keep my mouth shut, but at the end I held up my hand.

Dankins called on me and noted, "This is going to be the last word, people. This has gone on long enough. What do you have to add, Corny?"

"I agree with Vern," I said but no one laughed. "No, I just want to say that I agree with Joanne."

She turned around and looked at me, confusion and pleasure mixed on her plain face.

"That is to say," I went on, "there is a clear and present danger to the young people of this community. It is not the boy with wings, though. It's the people who want to sow seeds of fear everywhere, who try to make our young people believe that the whole world is like Blakesfield. Or worse, that the whole world is like one part of Blakesfield, the white, Christian part. That anyone who is different is dangerous and needs to be stomped on. That is the danger. People like Joanne talk about God creating the world and everything in it, and as soon as they see something or meet someone who isn't exactly like their puny little vision of the way things are supposed to be, they get all tied up in knots."

Joanne shot up but Dankins told her to sit down.

"Y'all know me," I looked around, "and y'all know I'm a mess. But I grew up here and I love this place. But this place sure as hell ain't all there is. And the sooner our kids realize that, the better and safer – yes, safer! – they'll be."

I looked around the room and saw a few heads nod and a few mouths tighten.

"With that," I said to the town manager, "I'll pass."

The end result of that two and a half hours of meeting was, as I had expected, pretty much nothing.

The supporters of the petition had spoken, as I said, loudly and at length, but in the end they had no specific recommendations to make. The council agreed to discuss it at a later time and report back to the community, Rob Dankins struck the table with his gavel and declared the meeting over and everyone staggered out.

Joanne and her crowd had not carried the day, but I heard plenty of unrest among people as they piled out and headed for their cars. Any number of people who had kept their thoughts to themselves at the meeting were obviously of the opinion that maybe something ought to be done. But what and by whom, no one knew.

I was getting on my bike when I caught sight of Hank, Sr. getting into his SUV. I raised my hand to wave but he turned his head and spit on the ground. Hank hadn't said anything one way or the other at the meeting. From what Katie had said, I thought Hank, Jr. was not a big Angelo fan, and I suspected that her friendliness toward the boy with wings did not count in his favor with Hank, Sr. either.

I pedaled back home under starry skies.

Chapter 16

The next morning was the last day of Vacation Bible School. Katie told me there would be awards – everyone got a ribbon for something – and then they would all go out to Peck's Park for the picnic that was the highlight of the week.

Peck's Park wasn't all that far from our house. It had been built with money donated by my mother in memory of her parents. There was a brass plaque on a granite slab at the entrance to the park that bore their names: Albert Joseph and Muggie Minerva Peck. I had only the vaguest memories of my grandparents, who had died in an automobile accident in Shamrock when I was four. Peck's Park was dedicated the next year, and I remembered sitting in the hot sun, wearing a stiff white shirt, black pants and a black bowtie that my mother had fussed with while I complained and tried to fight her off. Daddy finally took charge, swatted me a few times on the rear end and tied the tie around my neck. I sniffled through the whole ceremony and determined to hate the park forever.

The day of the picnic was hot, too, but not too bad by Blakesfield standards for late August. Most importantly, I didn't have to wear a tie. I put on jeans and a clean Dallas Cowboys tee shirt, packed some food for Billy Bob and tucked him into his stroller. I added a brown paper bag with a sandwich and an orange for myself and stuck a bottle of water into the pouch hanging on the back of Billy Bob's stroller. I pushed it along the side of the road and Billy Bob babbled away.

I used the time to try to get him to say "Katie." I was hoping to spring it on her as a surprise, but he refused to cooperate.

When we got to the park, the church vans had already pulled up and people were unpacking food and setting it out on long rows of tables under the cover of the pavilion. Kids ran here and there, squealing and laughing. I saw Hank and Hank, Jr. unloading a big cooler filled with cans of store-brand soda. Miss Missouri caught sight of me and waved. Wayne was there, too. Tiny's was providing hamburgers and hot dogs. I waved at him, but he was busy trying to get a portable steam table set up.

I looked around and finally saw Katie. She and Belinda were helping set out food. I pushed Billy Bob over, told the girls they were doing a good job and asked them to keep an eye on the baby. Belinda bent down and began cooing at him.

There were almost as many adults as there were kids. All the preachers were there, even Fr. Hickey, the old Irish missionary who said Mass at St. Maura Mission every other Sunday. Otherwise it looked like mostly women, as it usually is at church events. Men may insist they are in charge but I notice they tend to want the women to do most of the actual work. There were a couple of older men and Hank, deacons or some such thing I guessed. Hank, Jr. was too old to go to Vacation Bible School, but it looked like his father had roped him into helping with some of the heavy lifting. After unloading the cooler, the two of them started pulling stacks of folding chairs out of the back of their van.

Miss Missouri called my name.

"Corny, come help get these chairs set up, please."

Hank looked up and frowned, and I saw him say something to his son. Hank, Jr. looked at me with an evil grin. His father barked a command and they got back to work.

Miss Missouri knew that Hank and I were not on speaking terms, but it was just like her to try to put us in a situation where we would have to talk. I decided to try to work around her plot.

"Yes, ma'am. Where do you want the chairs?" I asked, picking up one in each hand and looking at her expectantly.

She glanced at Hank and said, "I'll leave that up to you and Hank."

She smiled sweetly and walked away.

Trapped, I turned and grunted, "Hmmm?"

Hank slammed the rear doors of the van and told Hank, Jr. to go help finish setting out the food. Then he turned to me with a stony face.

"I'm going to put some up over there in the shade. You can put yours where you want. I suggest someplace that the sun don't shine."

I think I mentioned that he had overcome his gentlemanly upbringing.

I might have made an ungentlemanly reply, but at that moment a shout went up on the far side of the park and all eyes turned in that direction.

A crowd of kids was standing by the swings and pointing. I looked and saw Angelo, hovering in the air. His white wings flapped slowly but powerfully as he sank down and rose up. Several gasps erupted behind me. I was sure there wasn't a person there who hadn't heard about the boy with wings, and quite a few had caught a glimpse of him. Seeing those wings rising above his bare shoulders was startling enough, but that was nothing compared to the sight of seeing him in actual flight, I realized. I don't know what I thought it would look like. I had not expected it to be so smooth, so natural or so beautiful.

"Angelo!" I heard a delighted shriek burst from Katie and saw her run across the packed dirt and dry grass of the park. Abandoning Billy Bob in his stroller, Belinda ran after her, calling for her to slow down.

Just at the edge of my vision, I saw Fr. Hickey crossing himself. Behind him, Joanne Smithers moved her lips rapidly but silently. Women clutched their hands to their chests, men stepped forward and then back, unsure what to do. Miss Missouri just stood and beamed. I wondered if she knew this was going to happen. Or maybe she had seen him fly before and was able to enjoy the sight without the haze of shock that confused the rest of us.

Katie had reached the crowd that stood under Angelo and was reaching up toward him. He began to move his wings more slowed and drifted down, touching first one foot to the ground, then the other. My daughter and Belinda rushed to his side, but I noticed the other kids held back. Most of them looked around at the adults, as if seeking instructions on how to act. I thought, *If we weren't here, they would act different.*

Katie had told me that all the kids in the park had played with Angelo, at least after their initial shyness had worn off. Hank, Jr. had teased her and Belinda, but as far as I knew, no one had bothered Angelo himself. To the kids, he was just another kid, one who happened to have wings.

But that was when there were no adults around. The easy equality of children playing among themselves dissolved in the presence of grown-ups. And not just any grown-ups. These were preachers and teachers and deacons, men and women of God. I remember when I was young thinking that God didn't seem to want me to have too much fun. I could see that vague thought flash across a number of faces in the crowd. Maybe it wasn't okay to play tag with a boy who had wings.

Joanne Smithers must have had all she could take. She stepped forward and called out, "Children! Children! Come back. It's time to eat. Come on, come back. We need to say a blessing. Who'll say the blessing?"

She looked around, seeking a supportive male face. She hesitated a few seconds over Fr. Hickey and then apparently decided she couldn't trust a Catholic grace. Langton Hughes was standing next to the Irish priest and she settled on him.

"Brother Hughes," she said, her voice shrill, "will you lead us in prayer?"

It was a rare preacher who could refuse a request like that, and he folded his hands and said loudly, "Let us pray."

The noise around Angelo continued for a moment, then softened, broke into sporadic whispers and died completely. A handful of faces turned toward Brother Hughes and a few of the younger kids steepled their hands together the way they had been taught in Sunday school. The older kids were quiet, but I noticed most of them were staring at Katie and Belinda, who had each taken one of Angelo's hands in their own.

A drawn-out hiss in my ear made me turn to my right. Hank, Jr. was staring at the girls and Angelo, his face red and tight. His father was standing behind him and reached for him just as Hank took off running. He managed to get a hand on his son, but the boy twisted and tore away. He put his head down and rushed toward Angelo.

Kids scattered to make way for the oncoming sixteen-year-old, and Katie and Belinda dropped Angelo's hands. It happened so fast no one could stop it, but there was a long second when we all held our breath, waiting for the impact.

But there was none.

One second Hank was about to butt Angelo in the chest and the next moment Angelo was hanging in the air ten feet above the ground, unharmed and apparently calm. He turned in the air to watch Hank, whose momentum carried him ten yards before he fell into a patch of Johnson grass at the edge of the park.

Hank rolled over and hopped up, dusting dirt off his jeans. I heard a snicker start among the kids, nervous laughter, but it stopped immediately when Hank glared over at the crowd.

Angelo had begun to come back to earth, but Hank picked up a nearby rock and hurled it at the descending figure. As smoothly as he had risen out of Hank's way before, Angelo lifted one wing turned to the side, letting the rock fly by. It hit the ground and bounced three times before stopping.

Hank picked up another rock and ran closer. The younger kids were running and crying, the older ones were shouting and the adults had finally started to move toward the action.

"Go away!" Joanne Smithers was shouting at Angelo. "This is all your fault. What if someone gets hurt? It will all be your fault! Get out of here! You aren't wanted around here!"

Hank stopped, a foot of two below Angelo's dangling bare feet. He jumped once or twice, trying to grab the feet, but he couldn't make it. Giving up on that, he took a firm stance with the rock gripped in his hand, drew his arm back as far as he could and yelled, "You heard her! Get out of here, you freak!"

We had all been staring at Hank and Angelo, but suddenly Katie appeared from nowhere and landed on Hank's back, beating him with her thin arms.

"Leave him alone!" she screamed. "Leave him alone!"

Her attack surprised Hank into dropping the rock and he was spinning around trying to dislodge her. She had one hand over his eyes and he couldn't see where he was going. She kept him blinded with one hand, whether intentionally or not was unclear, and beat on him with the other. All the while Belinda circled and circled them, trying to figure out how and whom to help.

Hank stumbled back against the frame of the swings and fell, twisting as he did so in such a way that he threw Katie free. He tried to regain his balance, but tripped on the rock he had thrown at Angelo before and went down. He hit his head on the corner of a picnic table and lay quiet. A red line began to drip down the side of his face.

Belinda began to scream.

That's torn it, I thought, echoing some old movie.

The smaller kids were already yelling and Belinda's screams inspired them to greater volume, tears and cries of "Mommy! Mommy!"

I ran toward Katie but found myself shoved roughly aside by Hank, Sr. on his way to his son, alternately roaring and swearing a blue streak that I would have found admirable had I not been so worried about my daughter at the time. I never would have suspected Hank had such a vocabulary.

Katie was lying on the ground on her back, chest heaving. Miss Missouri and I reached her at the same time. The old woman touched Katie's arm gently and said in a soft voice that was barely audible in the uproar that surrounded us.

"Katie, sweetie, are you all right?"

For a moment, all was quiet. I realized later that the chaos had continued unabated, but at the time it was as if the three of us knelt in a bubble of silence. I was examining my fallen daughter for blood stains but found nothing alarming. It seemed forever before she opened her eyes and spoke. Miss Missouri told me later it had been less than five seconds.

"I'm okay," she said, wiping dirt from her mouth and pushing herself up.

I hugged her so tightly that she winced, and I pulled back.

"You're hurt!" I said. "That son-of-a …"

I turned angrily around to yell at Hank, Sr. but when I saw him bent over his son, the words died in my throat.

Hank looked like the male version of the Pietà, holding his limp son half on his lap and rocking him back and forth. The blood that had been a trickle on Hank, Jr.'s face was flowing faster and Hank, Sr.'s pale blue shirt bore streaks of a dark, ominous hue.

He opened his eyes and looked at me, then at Katie, and his face twisted into rage.

"My son!" he shouted at me. "You took everything from me, you drunken scum. Couldn't you leave me my son?"

Miss Missouri reached out and touched my arm. The hair on the back of my neck prickled and my skin went clammy. I looked at father and son and my heart nearly stopped. What had Katie done?

Dawneen Phillips, one of Miss Missouri's daughters, showed up and calmly took charge of Hank. Dawneen was a nurse and I had heard that she had emergency room training. She had gone as a volunteer to a mission hospital in the Mideast during the last outbreak of violence, and she had seen such scenes all too often. But it prepared her to deal with it when the rest of the adults were paralyzed.

Fr. Hickey had called 911 and Hank had barely let Dawneen take over, checking for vital signs, before the ambulance pulled up. Fortunately the Cherokee Creek EMTs had been nearby, and with their arrival, a palpable sense of relief flooded the scene.

Miss Missouri poked me and I turned my attention back to Katie.

My daughter was rubbing her left arm, but she seemed unharmed. I was sure she would be bruised, but that was nothing compared to what might have happened to Hank, Jr.

Katie's rubbing and sniffing stopped abruptly as she caught sight of the ambulance.

"Is Angelo hurt?" she cried, looking desperately around. "Where is he? Did Hank hit him?"

She tried to rise to her feet, but Miss Missouri took her hand and held on to her.

"Angelo is fine," she said.

I had forgotten Angelo in all the fuss and looked around. He was nowhere in sight. I looked up into the sky, but the noonday sun's glare made it hard to see anything in the bleached blue overhead.

"Well, why is there an ambulance?"

Miss Missouri held her hand tighter.

"Hank didn't hurt Angelo, Katie. But he hurt himself when he fell."

"Good!" my sweet little girl said fiercely. "He deserved it."

Afraid that someone might hear her, I looked around. Fortunately almost everyone was crowded around the edge of the pavilion, trying and failing to stay out of the way of the EMTs who were loading a stretcher into the back of their green and white van.

With relief I saw that Hank, Jr.'s head was bandaged but he was clearly alive. His father hovered, anxious and babbling while Langton Hughes and Fred Phillips stood beside him, each with a hand on Hank's shoulders. They both looked calm and for a moment I was grateful for their reassuring presence. I had no use for preachers most of the time, and I doubt I would have found what they were saying to Hank very consoling had I been in his position. But Hank was a man of faith and it probably helped him. And that was what mattered.

Hank climbed into the back of the ambulance, the doors were closed and it sped off, siren screaming.

Those of us who were left looked at one another, stunned.

Dawneen had stayed behind and stepped into the breach.

"Well, I think these kids still need to be fed. Why don't we get everyone in line ..."

She and her mother enlisted the help of a few parents and clergy and they restored a semblance of normality. It was a quieter picnic than usual and it didn't last long. Katie and Belinda sat alone at a table with me until Miss Missouri and Dawneen were free to come join us. They tried to distract the girls by fussing with Billy Bob, but Katie didn't respond. She stared at the sandwich on her plate. She had taken one bite and put it down. From time to time she looked up and her eyes searched the skies.

Angelo was nowhere to be seen.

Chapter 17

The rest of Friday and all of Saturday passed in a slow dull ache. Contradictory reports about Hank, Jr.'s condition circulated through town, accompanied by wildly inaccurate descriptions of what had happened at the park. Angelo had picked Hank up and flung him into the picnic table. Hank had been trying to stop Angelo from dragging off a screaming six-year-old. Hank, Sr. had pulled a gun and taken a shot at Angelo and the bullets passed right through his body without harming him. Another version of the gun story had Angelo disappear in a puff of red and black smoke.

I kept Katie in the house and tried to interest her in a game of Go Fish, but she couldn't concentrate. She kept wandering over to the window and looking out. Belinda called three times but Katie didn't want to talk to her. Margaret Scranton called and told me the stories that were going around and asked me what had really happened. I was touched that she thought I would be a reliable witness.

When I finished my version, she said, "That's what Belinda says happened. It's a terrible thing, but why people have to make it worse is beyond me. Thanks, Corny. Next time I hear one of the horror stories, I'll see if I can offer a more reasonable perspective."

"That would be good," I said. "How's Belinda doing? Katie's in a state of shock, I think, whether more because of what happened to Hank, Jr. or what happened to Angelo, I'm not sure."

There was a long pause before Margaret responded.

"Belinda's okay. Do you think Katie might blame herself for what happened to Hank, Jr.? I mean, they were fighting when he fell."

I felt the blood rush to my face and took a deep breath.

"It was not her fault," I said tightly, "but I am sure she's blaming herself. She hasn't talked to me about it yet. She isn't talking much at all."

"Well, tell her we're praying for her. And for Hank, Jr. of course. And for Angelo."

As I hung up the phone, I thought again, *Margaret Scranton is a rare and good woman.*

Even as I had that thought, I remembered that I had not called Wayne to talk about the exercise he gave me to stop obsessing about Angelo. There was so much drama that I had not had time to call him or for that matter to obsess about Angelo.

I paused.

Why hadn't I obsessed about Angelo? If anything, the situation was worse than it had been all those days that I had been fretting about him. And I did think about him, wondered where he was, wondered if we would see him again. But it was a different kind of wondering, not burdensome, not lingering but passing naturally on to other concerns about Katie and about Hank, Jr.

Hank, Jr.

I had not thought to ask Margaret if there was any news. She would have been a reliable source, I was sure of that. Maybe Miss Missouri knew something.

"Katie, I'm going to go see Miss Missouri for a minute," I said, "Are you going to be okay?"

She nodded silently and kept looking out the window.

"If Billy Bob wakes up, you go take care of him, okay? I'm counting on you."

She nodded again but said nothing. As I was leaving the room, she pulled a chair over to the window and sat down where she could look outside.

Miss Missouri opened the door almost before I finished knocking.

"Come in, Corny. How's Katie today?"

I followed her into her dining room and we sat at the table.

"Want some coffee? Sweet tea?"

"No, thanks," I said. "I'm not thirsty. What I want is to know if you have heard anything reliable about Hank, Jr.'s condition. No one talks to me much but Margaret Scranton called to tell me some of the things she has heard around town about what happened. I forgot to ask her about Hank."

Miss Missouri rolled her eyes.

"You know that saying about Texans not lying, don't you?"

"That we just tell more truth than there is? Yes, ma'am."

"It's funny the first time you hear it and then you notice that it's not always funny in real life. I never heard so many stories in my life, and if I were a swearing woman, which you know I am not, Corny Shane, I would swear I must have been at a different picnic than all those other people, judging from what people are saying happened."

"I know, I know. But what about Hank, Jr.? How is he?"

Miss Missouri shook her head, her face sagging.

"Dawneen tells me that he is still in a coma or something like that. There's no news. And Hank and Chanice aren't letting anyone see him except immediate family, I guess."

I noticed my jaw was clenched tight and made a conscious effort to relax it.

"So what does that mean?"

"Dawneen says it just means the doctors wait. He may come out of it on his own. They ran all sorts of tests and haven't found anything necessarily deadly."

"Necessarily? Does that mean they found something?"

"Corny, I don't know. When Dawneen gets to talking medical stuff I get lost. And my memory's not what it used to be anyway. All I know is that we just have to wait. And pray. That's what I'm doing."

I thanked her and headed home.

I wasn't ready to pray. But maybe …

I remembered what Wayne had told me: Just say "Help" and "Thank you."

I looked up into the empty Texas sky.

"Hello, universe, it's Corny again. Help Hank, Jr. And Hank and Chanice. And Katie."

I walked on for a few steps before looking back up.

"And thanks. For taking away the obsession about Angelo."

I reached for the back door handle and looked up again.

"And help Angelo, I guess. I don't know if he needs help or not. But I thought I'd mention him, just in case."

I didn't know if that was praying or not, but it was what I did. I went back in the house to my silent daughter sitting by the window.

Chapter 18

It was the Sunday night following the picnic.

I hung around in the hospital lobby, half hidden behind a fake ficus in a corner and pretending to watch Fox News.

Why, I asked myself for the hundredth time, *did places like this think people wanted to watch Fox News?* Go into any fast food joint in Texas and odds were that blonde Fox News pretend-anchors would be glaring solemnly down on you. The food was greasy enough that what you really needed was something that would help digestion, not something that would increase the level of acid in your stomach, your heart or your brain. Give me re-runs of things like the old *Mary Tyler Moore Show* any day. At least Ted Baxter's foolishness was supposed to be funny, not deadly serious like so much of what passes for news reporting today.

Calm down, Corny, I said to myself. *Breathe in, breathe out. It's just television.*

I relaxed for ten seconds and then my irritation began to grow again. I was working myself up into a real stew when I happened to look out the big windows in the lobby. It was six o'clock and the sun wouldn't set for another two hours. In the glare outside, I glimpsed Hank, Sr. and Chanice walking across the parking lot toward their car. They must have gone out a side door, because I had not seen them come through the front. I waited until I saw the car bounce as it started and then pull out of the lot. I watched the tail lights grow smaller and then finally disappear around a curve half a mile away.

They're heading into town for supper, I thought to myself. Here's my chance.

I knew that Hank, Jr. was in Room 107. I had walked by it a dozen times in the last three days, but every time I had heard his parents' voices inside and couldn't work up the courage to go inside. I was in no shape to face them. I had asked at the front desk how the boy was doing, but the nurse told me that she could not give out any information.

"If you are a member of the family, I could page the doctor for you," she offered, concern on her dark face.

"No, just a … just a friend of the family," I said, realizing it was a lie.

I smiled and went to haunt the waiting area. I took out my cell phone and pretended to talk to someone. The nurse watched me for a moment and then went back to her papers.

Now that his parents had left, I nerved myself to look in on Hank. I knew from Miss Missouri that he had not come out of his coma. There was no sign of internal hemorrhaging, the doctors had told his parents, but he was not out of the woods. His pupils remained dilated and he had experienced a few seizures. These were all signs of potentially life-threatening brain trauma.

Although the doctors had said there was no reason to worry, Chanice had become hysterical at the news. She and Hank had separated the previous spring and she turned her anger on him.

"Hey," he yelled, loud enough to be heard at the nurses' station, "it wasn't my fault, bitch. It was a church picnic, for God's sake! If you want to blame anyone, blame Corny. That drunk is behind all our troubles. Back then, now, I guess forever."

It had taken the doctors and nurses some time to get them settled down, and Chanice finally had to be sedated. It had not been good.

But they had left together tonight, which meant they must have arrived together. One of those situations where tragedy brings people together, I thought, looking over my shoulder.

The nurses at the front desk had their backs turned. Putting my cell phone in my pocket, I coughed and strolled to the water fountain. I pushed the button and the metallic tang of Blakesfield's town water supply made me gag. The houses on Southwood Drive were outside the town water district, and I was used to the taste of my own well. I took a breath, bent my head and pretended to take a long sip.

When I turned around, they were still bent over some paperwork problem and tapping keyboards. I walked down the hall, past the restrooms, past the small chapel with its red cushioned pews and its backlit stained glass panel of a dove. I smiled to see it was a reproduction of the one in Bernini's *Gloria* in St. Peter's Basilica. There the light streamed through the white feathers of the Holy Spirit, poised above the baroque reliquary that held what some people believed was the original Chair of St. Peter. I wondered how the good Southern Baptists who had contributed to the building of this Chapel of the Holy Spirit would have felt if they knew that. Anti-Catholic feeling was not as strong as it had once been in this part of the Lone Star State, but it had not completely disappeared. These days it was mostly part of the distrust of Mexicans, of course. Anti-Catholic sentiment had a long history of association with anti-immigrant feeling in America.

Room 107 was three doors beyond the chapel, on the left. The first time I had walked by that room on Saturday night, there had been a *No Visitors!* sign in uncompromising red letters. The sign was no longer there, which I took to be hopeful. I paused outside the room and listened. The door was open two inches, but I heard no voices inside. Just the low hum of machinery. A respirator, I thought.

I walked a few steps down the hall and looked back through the door. There was a dim green light, but nothing else.

Glancing back to see if the way was still clear, I took myself in hand, pushed the door open and stepped inside. Behind me I pushed the door back, taking care to leave it open two inches, the way I had found it.

Hank, Jr.'s face was pale beneath his late summer tan. The green light from the panel above his head did nothing to make him look better. He lay with his head on a wrinkled hospital pillow, eyes closed. His chest rose and sank slowly. I glanced at all the numbers on the panel but couldn't make much sense of it.

I stepped closer.

"Hank," I said, talking to myself, not really to him.

"Hank, it's Corny. I just wanted to say I'm sorry. And to tell you that Katie's sorry, too. She didn't mean … well, she was just trying to protect Angelo, you know. Not to hurt you. And it was an accident."

I could hear a pleading note creep into my voice.

"I know you can't hear me. Well," I said, "maybe you can. I read somewhere that people in comas do hear what is going on around them. If you can hear me, I hope you can believe me. I wouldn't see you like this for anything."

And I meant it. He looked so much like his father at that age, back when he and I were inseparable companions. It was like looking at my best friend, lying in that bed, maybe in danger of never waking up.

"My best friend," I whispered.

I often heard people in meetings talk about how hard it had been for them to do the steps that involve making amends for the damage they had done to others. There are several steps in the process, including making a thorough self-examination, sharing what you discover with God (whatever that means to you) and another person, becoming willing to make direct amends and then doing so when it will not cause more harm to the person you hurt or to someone else.

My own sobriety was still too weak and fragile for me to think about making the kind of amend I owed Hank, Sr. And Chanice, for that matter. When I thought about doing that, I wanted to forget the whole thing. How could I face them after all this time? How could I expect them to forgive me?

"You can't expect them to forgive you," Wayne had told me in his rigorously honest way. "When the time comes to make your amends, we can talk about how you want to do it. But I will tell you this. You are the alcoholic, you are the one who did the damage, you are the one who needs to make amends. That is your job. Whether they forgive you or not doesn't matter."

"But that's not fair," I muttered.

"Welcome to the real world," he said. "It's not about what's fair. It's about what's right. These are your steps. Hank and Chanice, well, they're on their own journey. And whatever that is, it's not about making you feel good."

I remembered that as I stood at the foot of Hank, Jr.'s hospital bed, watching the respirator pump up and down, up and down. Green lines of light flowed across the panel, spiking and dropping, spiking and dropping. Numbers increased and decreased and then held steady.

How could anyone mend this?

I must have stood there without thinking much longer than I would have guessed. What brought me up short was Hank, Sr.'s voice in the corridor. I peeked out the door and saw him at the nurses station. I slipped out of the room and walked quickly toward the opposite end of the corridor. I ducked down a side hallway, found a stairwell and went down to the basement. Another long hallway filled with harsh fluorescent light led to an illuminated exit door. A sign beside the door read "Visitor Parking Lot."

I made my escape and rode my bike home.

When I got back to the house, there was an unfamiliar car parked in Miss Missouri's driveway. It had out-of-state license plates, looked like Oklahoma, but I didn't want to walk over and see. I put my bike away and went into the house.

When I took off for the hospital, I had left Katie and Billy Bob next door, and Miss Missouri hadn't said anything about expecting company. I decided to give her a call and tell her I was coming to get them out of her way.

Her phone rang three times before Miss Missouri picked up.

"Miss Missouri," I said, hearing laughter in the background, "I just got back. I'll be right there to get the kids. I'm sorry if they've been any trouble. Looks like you have company."

"Oh, Corny," she said, "can you … Hang on."

The phone got that muffled sound it gets when someone puts a hand over the speaker part. A minute passed before she came back on the line.

"Corny, I'll come over there first, okay? I have something to talk about with you and I'd rather do that in private."

I frowned.

"Okay, but you know I don't like to leave the kids unattended."

"That's … that's okay. A friend of mine is here and she'll be more than happy to keep an eye on them. More than happy."

"Is everything okay, Miss Missouri?" I asked. "You sound a little, I don't know, discombobulated."

She gave a nervous little laugh.

"I'm fine, Corny. And the kids are fine. Really fine. You wait for me and I'll be right there."

She clicked off and I put the phone back in its holder.

She was knocking at the back door almost before I had time to look out the kitchen window. I opened it and invited her in.

"What's up?" I said.

"Well," she sat down at the table, "first things first. What happened at the hospital?"

I gave her a brief account of my visit to Hank, Jr.'s room, omitting the details of what I had said to him. I was a little embarrassed about that, what I had said and that I had said it to someone in a coma.

Miss Missouri nodded but didn't say anything.

"I believe," I prodded, "that you said you wanted to talk to me about something? Was it just to hear about my trip?"

She shook her head vigorously from side to side.

"No, no! Not … not just that. But I did want to hear about it."

She stopped. I waited. I could hear the kitchen clock ticking away the seconds.

"Miss Missouri?" I prodded again.

She jumped.

"I'm sorry, Corny. I guess I am a bit discombobulated. It's about … it's about my company."

I nodded.

"I saw the car. Who is it?"

She took a deep breath.

"It's LuNella."

The room went black for a moment.

Chapter 19

An hour and a half later, Katie and Billy Bob were in bed. I had calmed down enough to go with Miss Missouri back to her house, where we found LuNella in a rocking chair, humming to a sleeping Billy Bob. Katie was staring at her mother, eyes wide open and face flushed. When we walked in, LuNella and Katie both turned to look at us.

"LuNella," I said, quietly.

"Corny," she answered and looked back down at Billy Bob, shifting his weight slightly in her arms.

"How've you been?" I asked.

Miss Missouri had already told me that LuNella had left the typewriter salesman somewhere out west When she heard about what happened to Hank, Jr. from one of the friends she still talked to in Blakesfield, she decided to pay a visit. Miss Missouri had looked down when she related that part and I was reasonably sure she was the friend in question. Part of me felt angry that my neighbor had known where my wife was all this time, but I was so stunned at the development that I put that aside for later.

"Sad," LuNella said, still not looking at me. "You?"

"Sad, too," I said, "but sober."

She looked at me and tilted her head.

"I heard that and I can see it, too. You look good."

There were a dozen questions I wanted to ask, but none of them seemed like the kind of thing I wanted to discuss in front of Katie or Miss Missouri.

I cleared my throat.

"I … uh, I came to get the kids. It's getting close to bed time."

She heaved a deep sigh and hugged Billy Bob to her chest. "I know. Can I … can I come help put them to bed?"

I started to say no but caught Miss Missouri's look.

"Sure, I bet they'd like that. Wouldn't you, Katie?"

Katie, who had not made a sound since I came in, nodded her head.

It was an awkward little procession from Miss Missouri's house to mine. LuNella held Billy Bob and Katie held my hand. Nobody said a word until we were in the house.

For a few minutes, it was like old times. LuNella got Billy Bob cleaned up and tucked him into his bed. Katie got herself dressed and got into her bed. LuNella and I kissed both of them goodnight and closed the door, leaving it slightly ajar.

"Do you want … coffee? Sweet tea?" I asked, heading for the kitchen.

"Corny," she said softly.

I turned.

"I'm sorry, Corny. I'm sorry I ran off. I'm sorry I showed up without warning you."

I came towards her and held out my arms to take her, but she backed away.

"But I'm not here to stay."

That stopped me dead. The room didn't go black this time, but it felt like the floor dropped twenty feet from under me.

Somehow I made it to the kitchen, got two glasses out of the cabinet and filled them with sweet tea. We sat and talked for half an hour before she went back to Miss Missouri's. She told me she was staying there overnight. She planned to try to see Hank and Chanice the next day and then head back to Oklahoma. She had a summer job at a Target in Ponca City. She had found a job teaching in a small Christian school and had to be back for orientation. She was building a new life. One without the typewriter salesman, who, no surprise, turned out to be a con man.

And a life without me. Or her children.

"How can you do it?" I asked. "Not how can you do it without me. I get that. I really do. I've changed, LuNella, but we both know that my drinking wasn't all that was wrong between us. But the kids, Katie, Billy Bob? How can you …?"

He face tightened.

"Corny," she said, "you aren't the only one with stuff. I've got stuff. I'm in no shape to raise those kids."

I looked at her in disbelief.

"And you think your drunk husband is?"

She smiled.

"Not my drunk husband. But from what I hear, my sober ex is doing a fine job."

I shook my head.

"No, I have no idea what I'm doing! I really don't. If it weren't for Wayne and Miss Missouri and Belinda's parents …"

She reached across the table and put her hand on mine.

"But that's the point, Corny. You have Wayne and Miss Missouri and the Scrantons. I don't have anyone. You can't do it alone, but you're not alone. You can't do it, but y'all are doing it now."

She patted my hand and got up.

"Maybe someday it will be different. But not for now."

"What am I supposed to tell the kids?" I asked, standing up and following her to the door. "That their mother left them again?"

"You tell them their mother lives somewhere else for now, but that they live in her heart no matter where she is. And I'll be back."

I shook my head.

"I will be back, Corny. But there's no going back."

She patted my cheek softly and walked out into the dark.

It took all my focus not to pedal directly to Cherokee Creek and the nearest bar.

Wayne had told me that when he first got sober, he had been told that all he had to do was get to bed at night without taking a drink. He used to come home, take off all his clothes, climb into bed naked and watch television or read into the wee hours. It wasn't easy, it wasn't fun. But going to get a drink would have required getting out of bed and getting dressed again, and that was enough of a problem that at least he could stay in bed until the liquor stores and bars were closed.

That night I tried it. But first, I opened the refrigerator and pulled out that old bottle of Liberation Ale. I looked at it for a long time and then smashed the glass neck against the sink and dumped the contents. The noise woke Katie and brought her running.

"Daddy, what happened?"

"Nothing, Katydid. Don't come in here. I need to get a broom and sweep up some broken glass."

I found the broom, swept up the splinters and then ran a towel over the floor again and again. The smell of the ale was strong and I could see Katie sniffing the air.

"Daddy, are you okay?" she asked.

I knew what she meant.

"I'm fine, Katie. I just had to do something I should have done months ago. Don't worry about it. I didn't drink."

"Where's Mama?"

I didn't look at her.

"Mama's staying with Miss Missouri tonight. Tomorrow she has to go back to her job up in Oklahoma."

Katie looked hurt.

"She's leaving again?"

I pulled her to me and hugged her tight.

"She's leaving for a while. But she is leaving you and Billy Bob with me, and with Miss Missouri and with all the other people here who love you. And she told me she will be back. Someday."

Katie sniffled and shook in my arms, and I held her and sniffled and shook, too.

Finally I asked her, "Are you okay?"

"No."

"Neither am I, sweetie, neither am I. But we will be. We will be."

She pulled back, looked up and me and nodded.

I kissed her on the head and she went back to her room.

I finished cleaning up the kitchen and checked all the doors and windows. I stood at the back door for a long time, looking at the car in Miss Missouri's driveway. The windows at her house were already dark.

I went to my own room and took off all my clothes. I got in bed, pulled the covers up over my naked body and picked up the Big Book, which I realized I hadn't looked at since Hank, Jr. got hurt.

I thought, *If it worked for Wayne, maybe it will work for me.*

I turned to the section in the back of the book where people share their stories and began to read.

I guess it worked. At least I didn't drink.

But I didn't sleep a wink either.

Chapter 20

Monday brought no reports of any changes in Hank's condition. He neither improved nor declined.

LuNella came by the house before lunch to say goodbye. She had tried to talk to Hank and Chanice, but Chanice hung up on her and after that the phone rang and rang but no one picked up. LuNella kissed the kids goodbye, cried and hugged me, and got in her car and drove away.

At lunch Katie said she was worried because Angelo had not appeared at the park over the weekend. I figured she was trying not to talk about her mother. Angelo was a safer topic. For her and for me.

"And, Daddy," she confided, "people are blaming him for what happened. But he didn't do anything; he didn't do anything at all. Hank started it and all Angelo did was get out of the way. Even when Hank started throwing rocks at him, he didn't fight back."

"I know, honey. I was there, remember?"

"Then why are people talking like he did something? I mean," she screwed up her face, "we just had Vacation Bible School. And Jesus said something about turning the other cheek. That's what Angelo did. Well, he didn't turn the other cheek because Hank didn't hit him. But he just turned and didn't fight back. He did what Jesus said to do, I think. So why aren't people talking about that?"

I nodded.

"Well, Katydid, you might as well learn that people like what Jesus said a lot. Because it's beautiful and sounds good. But people aren't always so good at doing what Jesus said and they aren't always so good at thinking people who try to do what Jesus said are doing the right thing."

She looked at me with lowered brows.

"That," she said stiffly, "makes no sense."

I smiled and said, "I agree. But it's the truth. No matter how much they say or even think otherwise, most people, most Christians, don't think that they are supposed to turn the other cheek or forgive their enemies seven times seven times or … well, lots of things Jesus said."

"That's not right."

"Well, you have to admit, a lot of the things Jesus said would be pretty hard to do all the time. Like I noticed that although Angelo just moved aside when Hank was throwing those rocks, someone jumped on Hank's back and started hitting him."

Red rushed up her face and she looked away.

"I know," she said. "It was my fault that Hank got hurt, not Angelo's. If I hadn't jumped on him, he wouldn't have fallen and he wouldn't have hurt his head and …"

She started to cry and before I could reach over to hug her, she slipped off the chair and ran to her room.

Oh, boy, I thought.

An old country song sprang into my mind, a song about a woman leaving her husband to deal with two hungry children and crops in the field. I found myself humming it and improvising lyrics:

You picked a find time to leave me, LuNella,

A sensitive daughter

and a baby as well,

You picked a fine time to leave me, oh hell!

I continued humming as I washed up the plates. Then I took Billy Bob out of his high chair, checked to make sure he was dry and headed to the living room for a father-son nap. I figured Katie needed some time to herself.

And I had no idea what to say to help her.

Chapter 21

There was no news of changes in Hank's condition for the next few days. The doctors were non-committal, according to Miss Missouri's sources, but Hank, Sr. and Chanice were getting discouraged.

The Friday after the disastrous picnic, I was sitting in the living room staring out the window at nothing. Katie came into the room and plopped down on the end of the sofa and sighed. When I didn't react, she sighed again, more loudly.

I shifted in my chair and looked over.

"What's up, puddin'?"

"I think I should go see Hank, Jr. and tell him I'm sorry about what happened," she said, not looking up.

"That's sweet, but you know, I don't think that's such a good idea. Hank, Jr. doesn't look too good from what I hear, and it might just upset you. And he's still in a coma, so it won't do any good to tell him anything."

She sniffed.

"But that's why I think I have to go tell him. Before … before anything happens."

And before I had a chance to reply, she burst into tears, ran across the room and threw herself into my arms.

I held her until the storm subsided. Finally she pulled away from my damp tee shirt and wiped her nose with the back of her hand. I reached into my pocket, pulled out a clean handkerchief and gave it to her. She blew her nose, folded it and held it out for me to take.

"No," I smiled, "I think I'll let you keep that. You may need it again. Toss it in your laundry when you're done with it."

She stuffed it in the side pocket of her jeans and leaned up against me.

"Daddy, is Hank going to die? And if he dies, did I kill him?"

How do you answer something like that?

"Honey," I kissed the top of her head, "we all hope Hank is going to be just fine. He's a strong guy and the doctors say he will probably be okay when he comes out of his coma. We just have to wait. They're doing all they can. You know they brought in that guy from Houston and he's real famous."

She nodded.

"But it's been a week. A whole week!"

I thought she was going to start crying again but she held off.

"I know, and that must seem like forever to you."

Forever and a half to Hank and Chanice, I thought.

"But what if he dies, Daddy? Is it my fault?"

I rocked my daughter back and forth. I would have given anything if LuNella had been there. Having her mother run off had been a horrible thing for Katie. Now this happened and LuNella showed up and then ran off again. Katie needed a mother right now. Miss Missouri and Margaret Scranton had stepped in and helped a lot, but they weren't LuNella.

"Katie, we'll cross that bridge when we come to it. And everyone is hoping and praying real hard that we don't come to that bridge. Meanwhile, try to remember that what happened to Hank was an accident. He tripped on a rock that he dropped himself, a rock he was going to use to hurt someone else. You didn't make him trip, you didn't push him into the picnic table. It was all an accident. No one is to blame."

She sniffed.

"But when I go to the park, a lot of the kids look at me funny."

I stiffened.

"Are they saying you hurt Hank on purpose?"

She shook her head against my chest.

"No. They don't say anything, but I bet that's what they're thinking."

She pulled back.

"Daddy, I want to go to the hospital. I want to tell Hank I'm sorry. Even if it's not my fault, I'm still sorry. I'm sorry he got hurt. I was just trying to help Angelo, not hurt anyone. I was trying to keep anyone from getting hurt. I need to tell him that."

I held her for a moment and then helped her off my lap.

"I need to think about it," I told her. "You know, Hank, Sr. and Chanice don't like me very much, and I don't want to cause them any more pain right now than they already have. We can't make other people feel bad just so we can feel better. Understand?"

Wayne's voice echoed in my head: *It's not about making you feel good.*

"I guess," she said, but she didn't sound convinced.

"I'll go talk to Miss Missouri," I said. "See what she thinks about it. She's pretty close to the Ingrams, and she keeps close tabs on how Hank is doing. I think we can trust her advice, don't you?"

"Yes, sir," Katie said.

"Now you go wash your face and check on your brother. I'm going to go next door and talk to Miss Missouri."

Before I went next door, though, I stepped into the garage and called Wayne.

He picked up on the first ring.

"What's up, son?" he asked.

I explained Katie's request.

"Uh-huh," he said. "I can understand that."

"I can understand it, but I don't feel comfortable taking her down there. She's never been in a hospital as far as I can remember. I think seeing Hank with all those tubes and pumps and monitors will be too much for her."

Wayne paused.

"That makes sense, but you know she's what, eleven or twelve, Corny. She has to grow up sooner or later and it sounds like she wants to start. To me, that sounds like she is ready, even though it might be hard."

"Well, maybe. I don't think she knows what she's in for. I was shocked when I saw him and I've seen lots of sick people. I think she's been through enough. This whole thing has been hard on her, you know. She blames herself for what happened and she thinks some of the kids are blaming her, too."

"Has anyone said anything like that to her?" he asked.

"No," I admitted. "But that's what she thinks and that's just as bad."

He snorted.

"Worse, more likely. There are probably just as many kids who think she was brave to jump Hank, Jr. He has a rep as a bully, and seeing how he was acting at that picnic, I think he is one. Throwing rocks at that little flying kid! What was that all about?"

"I don't know. But what am I supposed to do about Katie? You know if I take her down there, Hank, Sr. and Chanice are going to be there. I saw the look Hank gave her at the picnic. He blames her, all right. And you know how they feel about me."

Wayne had a coughing fit and I held the phone away from my ear until it subsided.

"Sorry 'bout that. I should quit smoking. But anyway, who are you trying to protect here, Katie or yourself?"

I didn't like that question.

"Well, her, of course," I said, and knew it was only half true.

I sighed.

"And me, too," I muttered. "But I'm not ready to face them, Wayne. You know that. We've talked about it. There's too much emotion going on over what happened to Hank, Jr. It wouldn't be fair to bust in on them at a time like this. Doesn't the program say we shouldn't make amends if it is going to do more harm?"

There was a long pause before Wayne spoke again.

"I didn't know this was supposed to be your amend, Corny. I thought it was Katie's."

He had me there.

"But I don't know if it will do any good. And she's awful young to have to face the kind of anger we may run into in that hospital room."

"You'll be there, though. If things get too tense, you can just take her out of the room. "

"I'm not sure I'll be much help."

"Take someone with you," he suggested. "Someone that the Ingrams trust."

"Like Miss Missouri?"

"Sure, she'd be perfect. She taught all y'all. I bet even Hank won't act up in front of her. Ask if she will go in first and talk to them, tell them Katie feels terrible and wants to tell Hank, Jr. that she's sorry."

I nodded, then realized he couldn't see me.

"Yeah, that might work. I was on my way over to talk to her anyway. I bet she'll do it."

"There you go, then," he said. "Now go."

I gulped, "It all seems overwhelming, Wayne."

"One day at a time, one thing at a time. All you have to do is the next right thing. And that is going to talk to Miss Missouri. Then just the next right thing."

"Yeah," I argued, "but what's that going to be?"

"You'll know when you get to that point. You don't know now. You can't turn the corner until you reach it."

I laughed.

"Did you make that up yourself?"

"Nah, heard it from some old timer over to Davis once. Why he didn't just say don't cross the bridge till you get there, I don't know."

I remembered I had said that to Katie not ten minutes earlier.

"Okay, thanks. I'd better get over there and see if I can catch Miss Missouri before she starts her lunch. Talk to you later."

"Good luck," he said and clicked off.

Chapter 22

I poked my head back inside. I could hear Katie singing to Billy Bob in their room. I closed the door softly and picked my way across the back to Miss Missouri's house.

She took so long to answer the door that I thought maybe she wasn't at home. I could see her car was in the garage, but the garage door itself was closed. Maybe she was out somewhere with Wanda Mae or one of her daughters.

Miss Missouri and Frank had raised four daughters: Dawn, Dawneen, Dawnette and Dawnelle.

"Frank wanted to name our first girl after his mother," Missouri had confided once, "but there was no way I was going to give her the satisfaction. She and I never saw eye to eye on anything. Frank and I were arguing about it in the hospital and the baby reached out and grabbed his little finger. He looked at her and said, 'What about Rosie? Her fingers are so pink?' I was taking a class on the Iliad and Odyssey at the time, and the phrase 'rosy-fingered dawn' popped into my mind. That was Eos, you know, but that was too unusual. 'How about Aurora?' I said."

She laughed.

"Frank said that sounded like some Disney character. He was right, you know. That was the name of the princess in *Sleeping Beauty*. So I said, 'Let's keep it plain English, then. Dawn.' And he agreed. We liked it so well, we just kept naming the girls some version of Dawn as they came along."

She had heaved a sigh and looked off into the distance when she said this.

"It seemed like such a cute idea at the time. The girls, of course, hated it. They all wanted their own name. And Frank never could get them straight. Neither could anyone else, for that matter. I can't tell you how often Dawneen came home from school upset because a teacher had called her Dawn. And all down the line."

Just as I was about to turn around and go home, feeling a bit relieved to postpone things, the door opened and Miss Missouri stood there.

"Sorry to take so long, Corny. I was on the phone with Wanda Mae and she's harder to get rid of than pine sap in your hair."

"That's okay, Miss Missouri," I said, glancing at my watch. Maybe there was still a way out of this. "I didn't realize it's probably your lunch time. I'll come back later."

She held the door wider.

"Nonsense! You come in this house. I'm just going to heat up some leftover Frito pie in the microwave and that won't take but a minute."

I bowed to the inevitable and went in.

Miss Missouri kept her house warm even in the summer. When Frank was in his last illness, he always felt cold and they kept the house at 85 degrees year round. A month before he died, a group of friends from his old Masonic lodge had driven a hundred miles to pay a formal visit. The four old men all wore suits and ties, and Missouri said she was embarrassed at making them crowd into the bedroom in that heat.

"Frank wasn't in any shape for visitors," she said, "so maybe it worked out. They didn't hang around too long, although I did feel bad that they had come so far for so little. People are good, Corny. They really are."

"If you say so," I had said.

I stepped inside and Miss Missouri closed the door.

She headed into her kitchen and I heard the refrigerator door open.

"I'll just put some of this on a plate and let it sit out while we're visiting. Otherwise, as forgetful as I am, I'll forget to eat lunch."

I came around the corner and sat down at her dining room table. She busied herself for a moment, reaching down a white salad plate, shuffling around in a drawer until she found a serving spoon and then scooping some of the Frito pie out of the bowl sitting on the counter. Curly corn chips, dark chili filled with chunks of Vidalia onion, melted cheddar plopped onto the plate. She put plastic wrap back over the bowl, patted it down to get a good seal and put it back in the refrigerator.

When she opened the door, I saw that the bottom shelf was filled with small bottles of one of those supplements a lot of older people take when they don't eat properly. She favored a chocolate-flavored Boost.

I smiled. I remember once I asked her what she was having for supper and she said, "Oh, I think I'll just have some booze."

"Booze?!" I said, shocked.

"Not booze, you idiot. Boost! Boost!"

She started to close the refrigerator door, stopped and turned around.

"Can I get you something, Corny? Sweet tea? Coke?"

I shook my head.

"No, thank you. I just want to talk to you for a minute, if you have the time. Then I promise I'll let you get back to your Frito pie."

She closed the door and came to sit opposite me at the table.

"What can I do for you? If it's about LuNella, I don't know that I can tell you anything. You need someone to babysit?"

"Maybe later," I admitted, "but that's not the thing. And it's not about LuNella either. Katie wants to go see Hank, Jr."

She nodded.

"I think that's nice. Kids her age usually don't want to go see people in the hospital. I can remember a time when hospitals didn't like visitors under the age of twelve. You're raising a good girl there, Corny."

"She is a good girl. But I'm not sure it's a good idea. You know I snuck in the other night to see Hank, Jr. He's in that coma and there are tubes and wires and monitors. I'm not sure she's ready for that."

"Did you explain that to her?"

"Yes, but it didn't change her mind. She wants to talk to him, to apologize, to tell him she's sorry he got hurt."

"Again, you're raising a good girl there, Corny. As hard as it is to go see someone in the hospital, it's a whole lot harder to apologize for something. Especially if that something is the reason he's in the hospital to start with."

I flushed.

"You know, Miss Missouri, that it is not Katie's fault that he got hurt. He tripped and hit his head. And he tripped on a rock he had intended to throw at another person and hurt him."

She looked at me directly.

"Corny, you and I know that Katie didn't hurt Hank on purpose. But she feels bad because he got hurt and she wants to apologize for her part in that, no matter what she meant or didn't mean to happen. If you are asking my opinion, I think you should let her do that."

A phrase from something Wayne has said came back to me.

"It's all about cleaning up your side of the street, son. It don't matter if the other side is trashed, too. You can't do anything about someone else's stuff. But you can do something about your own."

I repeated that to Missouri and she smiled.

"Maybe there's more to that program of yours than I thought. Katie is trying to keep her side of the street clean. Maybe she is responsible for some of the trash, maybe circumstances blew some of it over there. But she wants to do the right thing. Let her do it."

I sat for a moment, clenching and unclenching my fist.

"You know that Hank and Chanice will not be happy if I show up at the hospital."

Missouri nodded.

"I know. I know," she said softly, reaching across and patting my fist. "Maybe … maybe the time has come for you to apologize?"

My face burned.

"I thought we said this was not about me."

She shook her head.

"I didn't say that. Did you?"

I thought about it a second.

"No, but Wayne said something about this being Katie's amend and not mine."

"And," she went on, still holding onto my hand, "maybe it is about Katie. But maybe it could be good time for you, too."

I shook my head.

"No, I tried. I tried back when all that happened. Hank's parents just hung up on me when I called, and he never answered any of my letters. That's a long time ago. I think it's best to let sleeping dogs lie. This is not about what I did or didn't do …"

She looked at me.

"Okay, this is not about what I did. It is about what Katie wants to do."

She patted my hand a few times and then drew hers back and let it fall into her lap.

"If that's the way you want it."

"That's not the way I want it. That's just the way it is. Now is not the time."

Sixteen years of anger boiled up. I clenched my fist again and spoke through gritted teeth.

"You know, Miss Missouri, Hank and his parents poisoned this town for me. They spread stories about what a terrible person I was, how I had ruined his life and Chanice's life. I was a drunk, or well on my way to one. But they hinted that I took drugs, that I sold drugs to other kids. When LuNella and I got married, Hank's mother got on the phone and tried to get a lot of the people we invited to refuse to go. People told me about those phone calls. And that was four years later. Talk about holding a grudge! And them so proud of being good Christian people. And that's how they acted. No wonder Hank couldn't forgive me, growing up surrounded by that kind of Christian love."

I stopped to catch my breath. Miss Missouri had not said a word. I went on.

"I know Hank and Chanice were hurt. But I was hurt, too. What do you think it was like being the guy who ruined his best friend's life? I couldn't wait to get out of this town, get away from the looks and the whispering. And not everybody whispered, you know! Not everybody ***whispered***."

She looked down at the table and sighed.

"One of the hardest lessons we all have to learn, Corny, is that actions have consequences. And we have to live with those consequences, even when they hurt and even when they seem unfair. Shoot, we have to live with them even when they ***are*** unfair."

She reached across and touched my clenched fist.

"Are you sure it's only the Ingrams who are holding onto something? You are sitting here in my house, at my table and your hand is clenched. I think maybe something inside might be clenched, too."

I pulled my hand away rudely.

"Maybe it is. But I have every right to have a grudge. I don't know, maybe that was one reason I became an alcoholic, you know? Maybe it's their fault."

She raised an eyebrow.

"Not your guilt? Or something else?"

I got up.

"I think I need to talk to Wayne again about what to do. I appreciate your time, Miss Missouri."

I saw the pain flash across her face, but it didn't matter. I turned and walked out.

I need a drink, I told myself as I walked across Missouri's yard to my own. I need a drink, I deserve a drink.

I stuffed my hands into my jeans pockets and my hand hit the coin I carried there.

You, Cornelius Barnabas Shane, need to talk to your sponsor.

Yes, I do, I thought. *But first, I need to turn around and apologize to that sweet woman I just insulted when all she was doing was try to help.*

I turned on my heel and went back. The door opened before I had a chance to knock.

"Oh, Miss Missouri, I'm so sorry. I don't know why I acted like that."

She folded me in her thin arms and patted my back.

"That's okay, honey. I know that wasn't you. That was the pain talking. And pain is a bad talker."

I hugged her tightly.

"Thank you. I'm going to call Wayne. I'll let you know how that goes."

"You do that," she said, releasing me.

"And Miss Missouri, can I ask a huge favor?"

"Anything," she said.

"If Katie and I go to the hospital, will you go with us? Maybe go in and talk to Hank and Chanice for us?"

"Let me think about that. Why don't you ask Wayne what he thinks."

"It was his idea," I admitted. "Sometimes I don't think all that clearly, even sober. I don't know what I'd do without him. Or without you, you know that."

"Honey, I don't know what any of us would do without any of us."

She smiled and closed the door.

I was halfway across the yard when I realized she had not agreed to go to the hospital yet. I started to go back but then remembered she had asked for time to think about it. I kept walking. One step at a time, I said, one step at a time.

Back at the house I went to check on Katie. She was standing next to Billy Bob's crib, singing nonsense syllables. He was looking at her like she was making the most sense he had ever heard in his life. I walked over and stood behind her. He looked up and stretched chubby arms toward me.

"Papa! Papa!"

Katie turned around.

"I've been practicing with him," she told me. "I think he's doing real good, don't you?"

I hugged her with one arm and reached my free hand out to my son.

"I think you're both doing real good. Real good. Real well, that is."

We stood there for a few moments in silence. Finally I let go.

"I need to call Wayne about something, okay?"

She nodded.

"What did Miss Missouri say, about me going to the hospital to see Hank?"

"She gave me some advice. It was very helpful but part of it was to talk to Wayne. So I'm going to go do that. You stay here and practice with Billy Bob. Why don't you teach him to say Katie?"

She grinned.

"I've been trying. No luck so far. All he does is say 'ka-ka' and that doesn't sound good."

I laughed.

"No, that doesn't sound good at all. Keep at it, kiddo. He'll catch on."

I went into the living room. From the kid's bedroom I could hear Katie saying her name over and over.

Next thing I know, she'll be teaching him to say Billy Bob wants a cracker, I thought.

I stepped out onto the porch to call Wayne. It was hot, but there was a breeze and in the shade it wasn't too bad.

"Pick up, Wayne," I chanted, hoping the magic words would get through. His phone rang five times and went to voice mail.

"Hey, it's Wayne," his message said. "Leave a name and number and I'll be in touch. Easy does it."

Wayne loved the slogans that the program had in abundance. *Easy Does It* was his favorite, which explains why it was on his phone message. But when he said it to me, he almost always amended it: "Easy does it, son. But do it!"

"Hey, it's me. I talked to Miss Missouri and she's thinking about helping us out. But she said something about maybe it being time for me to apologize to Hank and Chanice. I'm not comfortable with that. So give me a ring when you get a chance."

I clicked off and went back into the house.

Katie was shouting, "No! No! Not ka-ka! Not ka-ka!"

I could hear Billy Bob squealing with delight.

Yeah, that's the way to make him forget that word: say it loud and often, I thought and headed to their room.

Maybe the best way to suppress this behavior is to ignore it, I thought. *Not reinforce it by getting excited. I'll have to suggest that to Katie.*

Chapter 23

It was after eight that evening when Miss Missouri parked her car in the lot adjacent to the hospital.

Somehow it had taken longer to arrange for everything than I had expected. Wayne took a while to get back to me, but he encouraged me to go and see what happened. Then I had to get Katie and Billy Bob fed. My son must have sensed the tension because he was very uncooperative. I was happy when Russselene arrived and I could hand him over to the babysitter.

When I saw how late it was, I suggested to Miss Missouri that we wait, but she thought the time had come. Katie and I climbed into her car and rode to the hospital in silence.

While Missouri was putting her keys away, I hopped out and walked around to open the door for her while Katie climbed out of the back seat. Missouri patted me on the cheek and said, "Shall we go in?"

At the door, she took Katie by the shoulders and held her at arm's length.

"Katie, honey, you know I'm going to do what I can. I know this is important to you and I think you are doing the right thing. But the most important thing right now is that Hank's parents need our prayers and our love. We need to do what's best for them. So if they say they don't think they are ready, that will be okay. Do you understand?"

Katie nodded, "Yes, ma'am. I understand. Daddy told me to do the next right thing, and the next right thing is to ask. If they say 'no,' the next right thing will be to accept it. Right, Daddy?"

I nodded, my face blank and tight. I was proud of her and afraid for her.

Miss Missouri hugged her and walked over to the front desk to talk to the nurse. After a few sentences, the nurse looked our way and then back to Missouri. She nodded, Missouri turned and waved and headed down the hall.

Katie and I sat down in the visitors' area where I had waited five days before. I picked up a magazine and opened it at random. A blurry picture of Camilla, Duchess of Cornwall, filled half the page under headlines, "The Evil Camilla Tries Again!"

I closed the magazine and tossed it back on the table. I fished in my pocket for the silver-dollar-sized plastic disk I had carried for the past few months. I took it out and read the familiar words over and over: … *the things I cannot change, courage …*

Katie was sitting as still as a mouse, her eyes huge in her tan face. Her fingers were intertwined in her lap. She looked calm but white knuckles indicated how tightly her fingers were clenched.

… *the things I cannot change …*

Minutes passed. Five. Ten. I read all the posters on the wall, stared at the directory behind its glass cover. There were two large vending machines in a niche, one filled with soda and the other with candy, chips and plastic-wrapped sandwiches. Taped to the pillar beside them was an announcement that the hospital was expanding and would soon have a coffee house and small food court.

A young Hispanic couple came in, a boy of about three clutching their hands. The parents let go of his hands and walked to the front desk.

The boy looked around, saw me and stared for a moment. Then he walked in that stiff gait of kids that age over to an area in the waiting area where a table covered with toys stood beside a box out of which peeked plush lions and giraffes, pigs and robots. He began digging through the box.

I poked Katie.

"He's been here before."

She glanced at him, said, "Hmmm," and then went back to staring at the floor.

A moment later, a door that led into a suite of offices opened and a tall, thin woman in a long white coat came out. The Hispanic couple greeted her and their son turned. His black eyes lit up, he threw the plush lion back into the box and hopped and bounced across to the doctor.

I looked at his father and said, "He seems happy."

White teeth flashed in the brown face, and he said, "Yeah, he's pretty juiced."

They all disappeared through the door into the offices and the lobby was quiet again, except for the distant ringing of a telephone.

Katie sat still but I was growing restless. I stood up and stretched, walked to the windows and looked out at the parking lot.

"Corny?" Miss Missouri's voice broke my trance.

I turned around and Katie got up.

"Well," Missouri told us, "they are willing to let Katie come in. Hank didn't want to let you come, Corny, but I pointed out that it was not fair to Katie to make her come in by herself. You can't stay for long, and I promised you would be brief. Okay?"

Katie nodded and took a deep breath.

"Well, let's go," I said, taking her by the hand and signaling for Miss Missouri to lead the way.

"Oh, I don't think I had better go. The room is not real big and there are … machines all around. The fewer people in there at a time the better for Hank, Jr. and for his folks, I think. I'll wait here."

She went to sit down but turned to look at us.

"Be brave, Katie. This is a very grown-up thing you are doing. I'm proud of you. And I'll be out here praying for you."

She looked at the magazines on the table, picked one up and sat in a chair near the large windows.

"Well, kiddo," I said, "looks like it's just you and me."

We walked past the little chapel and down to Room 107. The door was cracked open the way it had been when I visited Hank, Jr. on Sunday night. It seemed ages ago.

I tapped and heard Hank's strained voice say, "Come in."

"Ready?" I asked Katie.

She nodded and I pushed the door open. We stepped inside.

I caught a glimpse of Hank, Sr.'s anger and looked away. I kept my hands on Katie's shoulders, telling myself I was protecting her and not using her to shield myself. I almost believed it.

Hearing Hank, Sr. growl, Chanice looked up from a chair in the corner where she had been dabbing at her eyes. Her once pretty face was lined with worry, black eye makeup in streaks along her cheeks. The wrinkles in her clothes bore witness to how many hours she had worn them, maybe slept in them. A red blob of some indeterminate sauce marred the collar of her jacket. Slight smudges showed that she or someone had attempted to wipe it away, succeeding only in spreading the stain. She started to rise, then fell back, waving her hand in front of her face.

"I changed my mind. We're not ready for any visitors," Hank, Sr. hissed. "Especially … Just get the heck out."

He went no further.

Katie gulped and spoke up.

"Mr. Ingram, ma'am, I'm so sorry about what happened to Hank. I just wanted to tell him that I'm sorry, that I didn't mean for him to be hurt. I didn't want anybody to get hurt. It was all a horrible … horri…"

Her voice broke and she turned and buried her head against my stomach.

I cleared my throat and looked at Hank.

"Hank, I know this is a terrible time for you," and looking at Chanice, "and for you. It's a terrible time for all of us. The whole town is upset, you know that. And whatever may have happened in the past ..."

His eyes widened and his shoulders rose.

"Whatever ***did*** happen in the past, especially the pain that I caused you then and that my presence has continued to cause you, I apologize. I was wrong. I ruined my own life, you know that, destroyed my marriage with my drinking. But before that, I ruined yours by what I did. There's no way I can undo that, not after all these years. There never was a way to undo it, or I swear to God I would have found it. But I didn't, I couldn't. And someone I cared about more than anyone in the world suffered for it. I ... I guess I had to say that."

Hank looked at Chanice and then back at his son in the hospital bed, tubes and wires running from him to the battery of monitors. He did not look at me.

"I am not asking you to forgive me, although I wish that were possible. But I do ask you now to let Katie tell Hank she's sorry for what happened to him. I didn't mean to hurt you, Hank, or Chanice. But I did and it was stupid and even though I didn't mean to hurt you, what I did was my fault. I think I did it to hurt LuNella in some stupid teenage guy way, get back at her for ruining your graduation. And then I ruined a lot of other things for her. All those things were my fault, no one else's. I have to live with that and I deserve your resentment.

"But this is not Katie's fault in any way. She didn't mean for Hank to get hurt. You heard what she said. She didn't want anyone to get hurt. That's what she was trying to stop. She was just trying to protect a friend. Be magnanimous for her sake. Don't make her wait for years to apologize. Give her a moment, please. Just a moment. Now, not sixteen years from now. And I promise we will leave you alone."

I stood there, my heart pounding, for what seemed like forever. Finally Hank looked over at us.

"Katie, I'm doing this for you."

She turned to look at him and nodded.

"Thank you, sir" she whispered.

"Thank you, Hank," I echoed. "That's mighty big of you."

Then he raised his eyes to mine.

"But not for you. Never for you."

He went over to Chanice and spoke in a low tone. She shook her head and he spoke again. Finally she nodded and he helped her to her feet.

"Katie, Chanice and I are going to go outside and give you a little privacy. But that door will be open and we will have our eyes on you. I don't want you to mess with any of the things in here, okay? You've done … Hank has suffered enough. But you can come over and talk to him."

He looked at a clunky watch on his wrist.

"One minute," he said. "Starting now."

He and Chanice brushed past me, Hank bumping against me and pushing me into the wall on his way out the door.

Katie walked over and stood by the bed, looking at Hank, Jr.'s face, green in the glare of the monitor lights.

"Honey, you only have a minute. Say what you want to say and let's leave the Ingrams alone. I promised. Let's not make them wait."

She nodded and opened her mouth to say something.

But just then we heard a knock on the window.

Chapter 24

We both jumped and looked out. Angelo was outside, wings gently holding him aloft, inches from the window. He looked at Katie and tapped again on the window.

As far as I knew, no one had seen Angelo in the past week. In the turmoil at the park, he had simply disappeared. We assumed he had flown away, perhaps frightened by Hank's attack on him. Now suddenly he was here.

My feet were rooted to the floor, but Katie was moving towards him.

"Katie, wait!" I tried to shout, but it came out as a croak.

She kept moving and I looked back at the door. I could see Chanice and Hank across the hall, absorbed in their own conversation. Hank's eyes were fixed on the door, though, and I saw him straighten up when he glimpsed Katie moving out of his line of sight.

When I looked back, she was at the window, fumbling with a latch. The window swung open and somehow Angelo was in the room. How he managed to get those wings folded in close enough to his thin body to get through the narrow window, I could not see. He was outside, wings spread and then he was inside, bare feet touching down onto the floor. He took Katie's hand and they smiled at one another. He looked at me, then at Hank and moved to the bed. I heard the door creaking behind me and moved instinctively to block the way.

"What the …?" Hank roared as he came in, Chanice crowding and whimpering behind him.

"What's wrong? What happened?" she said, pushing Hank aside to get a view of the bed where Angelo and Katie stood.

Angelo reached out and lay his palm on Hank's head, gently, like a feather floating to earth.

"Get your hands off him, you damn freak!" Hank shouted and reached into his pocket.

Everything went crazy.

Hank's body jerked, the lights in the room dimmed and brightened, monitors flat-lined, then began peaking and dipping, alarms rang.

Hank, Jr. opened his eyes, looked into Angelo's eyes and grinned. He turned his head to the side.

"Dad?" he said.

A blast from behind deafened me and the window exploded into millions of glittering bits of light. At the same moment a burst of white feathers flew out amid a fine spray of red drops. Katie screamed and fell to the ground.

Nurses came from nowhere, small furies who shoved Hank, Chanice and me aside. Dawneen Philips ran to the bed and looked at Hank, Jr., at the monitors, back at the boy. He smiled at her.

"Hey! What happened?" he asked her.

Another nurse bent next to Katie, who lay in a crumpled pile against a wall. There was a hole in the wall above her, and there was blood on the splinters of glass littering the floor. I tried to get to her but tripped over a bundle of cables spilling out from under the bed.

"Everyone out! Out!" said the nurse by the bed.

Two stout orderlies had come in and they began to hustle the three adults through the door. Chanice was in hysterics and Hank looked stunned. I realized that a gun was clutched in his right hand, dangling limply at his side.

A gun. Of course. We were in Texas. Someone was bound to be carrying a gun.

Outside the room, two security personnel were waiting. The woman took charge of Chanice, leading her to a row of chairs in the hallway and trying to calm her down. Miss Missouri had come running when she heard the noise. She sat down by Chanice, wrapped her arm around her and rocked her like a child, murmuring and patting her head.

The security man calmly asked Hank to give him the gun and held out his hand. Hank looked at the gun blankly for a moment. Then his chest heaved and he passed it to the officer..

He didn't look at me, but he whispered, "I didn't mean to hurt Katie, Corny. I would never hurt Katie."

"I know that, Hank," I said numbly to the man who used to be my best friend, the man who had hated me for the past sixteen years, the man who had just shot my daughter. "I know you wouldn't."

"Come with me, please sir," the security man said politely and took Hank by the arm. Turning to me, he said, "Wait here. Do not leave. George," he looked at the larger of the orderlies and nodded at me, "stay with him."

George nodded and looked grim. The officer and Hank disappeared down the corridor.

Nurses, orderlies and janitors were rushing in and out of Room 107. I looked at George and asked if I could sit down. He pondered for a moment and then nodded.

"We have to stay here in the hall, though," he said as I moved toward an empty chair next to Missouri.

She looked up and shook her head slightly. She held Chanice's head to her shoulder so the weeping woman couldn't see me approaching.

"I'll just take this chair over there," I whispered and started to drag it.

The chair looked flimsy but it was heavy and made a screeching sound when I moved it. George jumped over and lifted it easily. He took it down the hall about ten feet and placed it against the wall. He hooked a finger and me and pointed to the chair.

"Sit."

I sat.

I was still in shock from what had happened, and I was anxious to know how badly Katie had been hurt. I felt for the plastic coin in my pocket and twiddled it between my fingers.

Accept the things … No! Don't make me accept that.

Even as I thought it, I realized that my agony over my daughter had lasted less than five minutes. Hank and Chanice had been going through hell for the past week. I had felt bad for them, but until this moment I had no idea what they have been feeling.

Another ten minutes passed and the nurse I didn't know came out leading Katie and looking around. Miss Missouri caught her eye and pointed down the hall toward me. Katie yelled, "Daddy!" and tried to run, but the nurse held her arm and made her walk more slowly.

"You're okay, young lad," she said firmly, "but this is still a hospital."

I stood and walked over to Katie, who threw her arms around me and squeezed and squeezed. George had come over with me, but he stood back to give us space.

"Is she okay?" I asked the nurse. "I saw … there was blood and …"

The nurse put on what I assume she thought was a reassuring smile. If that was what she thought, she was way off base.

"Nothing at all, nothing. There was a lot of glass from the broken window and she had some blood on her arms and legs. But when we got her cleaned up, there were no cuts. It wasn't her blood, I guess."

I frowned.

"Whose was it? Was Hank hit?"

If he had hit his son when he fired that gun, Hank, Sr. might never recover.

"No," the nurse shook her head. "He was fine, too. Amazingly fine, all things considered. That is one lucky boy. Katie says that there was another boy there, an Angelo?"

She looked a question at Katie who nodded and sniffed.

"Yes, Angelo. I saw him."

A sick feeling rushed over me. There had been blood and a shower of feathers.

Angelo.

"Well, I don't know about that. He's not there now. No one is there. And no one came out of the room. As soon as we heard the shots, Nurse Philips and I came running. And when the custodial staff cleaned the room, they swept under the bed and in the closet and in the bathroom. There was glass everywhere! But there was no Angelo or anyone else in that room. Just Hank, Jr. and Katie."

I looked at Katie.

"Katie, what happened to Angelo?"

She shook her head and wiped her eyes.

"I don't know. He touched Hank and then Hank woke up and then there was a noise and the window exploded and someone was screaming. I think," she looked embarrassed, "I think I may have fainted. The next thing I remember is the nurses asking if I was okay."

I held her at arm's length and spun her around slowly.

"Hold out your arms," I told her and she obeyed.

"Show me."

I examined her arms, her head, her neck, her tanned legs. There were no marks anywhere.

"Where did the blood come from, then?" I asked the nurse. "There was blood wasn't there? I know I saw blood on her."

The nurse nodded.

"There was blood. Or," she became cautious, "there was something red. But it wasn't Katie's blood and it wasn't Hanks."

"Can she go home?" I asked.

"Oh, sure! All she needs is a good night's sleep."

Katie laughed.

"I don't think I'll get any sleep, but I do want to go home."

Chapter 25

As she said this, Dawneen Philips and an orderly pushed a gurney through the door. Hank was lying on it, eyes open and looking calm. Dawneen saw her mother with Chanice and signaled the orderly to wait. The gurney stopped a few feet away from where the two women sat. Chanice's head was still buried in Miss Missouri's shoulder, but the older woman whispered to her. Chanice leapt up and rushed to her son's side.

"Hank, Hank, baby, are you okay?"

She grabbed his right hand and clung to it.

Hank pretended to wince and said, "Easy, easy! I'm fine. They're taking me for a ride, I'm so fine."

Dawneen smiled and explained, "Hank is doing remarkably well. But Doctor Weller wants us to take him to intensive care for observation. We want to keep an eye on him overnight, make sure things stay stable."

Hank looked over and Katie and winked.

"I've never been stable before, huh, Katie? Not sure why I should start now."

She leaned into me but didn't reply.

"Let's go, young man," Dawneen said.

She and the orderly starting moving the gurney and Chanice walked along side, never releasing Hank, Jr.'s hand. They turned a corner halfway down the hallway where it intersected with another corridor and disappeared.

Miss Missouri rose and came over to me.

"Now what?" she asked.

She looked exhausted. I glanced at my watch and realized it was after eleven. Miss Missouri was probably the early-to-bed, early-to-rise sort. She and Katie both looked like they needed to get to bed. And for the first time since excitement in Room 107, I realized that Russelene was still at our house with Billy Bob. She needed to get home, too.

"Let me call Russelene," I said, "and we'll get you both home."

I was pulling my phone out of my pocket when George coughed.

"I'm sorry, but I don't think you can take them anywhere. You have to stay here until security or the police say you can leave."

In my relief at being reunited with Katie and seeing Hank's amazing recovery, I had forgotten for the moment that I was being held.

"Why do I have to stay?" I asked angrily. "I didn't do anything."

"Those were my orders. You stay and I stay with you."

I looked at Miss Missouri.

"Okay, first things first. Let me call Russelene and tell her what's going on. She must be worried sick."

"Maybe," Katie said, "but she didn't call you, did she?"

I looked down and saw that my phone was turned off. When I clicked it on, I saw that I had missed three calls. All from the babysitter.

Russelene answered her phone on the first ring, and I could tell by her voice that she had been anxious.

"Oh, Mr. Shane, I didn't know what to do. I didn't want to bother you and I knew you were at the hospital and Billy Bob is asleep, he's so sweet, but it's later than …"

"Russelene, slow down. We're still at the hospital… No, everything's fine. But I'm going to be stuck here for a while and I don't know when I'll be able to come home. Do you think you could call your parents and see if you can stay later?"

"Well," she said, "I don't think they would want me to be out by myself all night or anything."

"Yeah, that makes sense. Miss Missouri's here with me. What if she brings Katie home, would your parents let you stay then? I know Katie's only eleven, but …"

Miss Missouri tapped my arm.

"Corny, tell Russelene I will bring Katie home in your car and I'll stay overnight with the kids myself. As soon as I can get there, Russelene can go home. But she needs to call her parents and tell them what's going on."

"Okay, thanks. Did you hear that, Russelene? Call your parents and tell them that I have to stay at the hospital for a while and that Miss Missouri will be coming over and let you go home in ten or fifteen minutes. And Russelene, I appreciate your doing this. I'll give Miss Missouri your money and there'll be an extra twenty in it."

Russelene promised to call her parents immediately, I clicked off and handed Miss Missouri my house keys and money for the babysitter.

"I owe you big time," I told her.

"That's what neighbors are for, Corny," she said, retrieving her purse from the floor beside the chair where she had been sitting. "You come home as soon as you can. I'll take care of the kids."

I hugged Katie and told her, "You help Miss Missouri with Billy Bob, okay? I'll see you in the morning. I won't have to stay long. They just want to ask me some questions, I think. I'm not in trouble. Nobody's in trouble."

I wasn't sure that was true. Hank had fired a gun in a crowded hospital room. But I didn't want to give Katie anything more to worry about.

I waved them goodbye and went to sit back down in the corridor to wait.

Chapter 26

An hour later the hospital security officer woke me from a fitful doze. I looked around and saw George wandering off to other duties and yawned.

"Mr. Shane?" he asked.

"That's me," I agreed, struggling to my feet. My shirt had twisted itself around under my arms and it took me a moment to make myself presentable.

"I'm Officer Wilton, head of security for the Blakesfield Area Hospital. Would you come with me, please, sir. This should not take long. Just a few questions."

I followed him down the corridor and through the door that led into the suite of offices by the waiting area in the lobby.

According to a clock on the wall, it was 2:15. There were a few lights on, but I didn't see anyone else until Officer Wilton pushed open a door and led me into a room where a few chairs sat around a rectangular table. A smaller table with a Keurig coffee maker and a stack of foam cups stood in a corner. A tray held packets of sugar and fake cream.

Hank, Sr. sat in one of the chairs, face worn and lined. He looked up when we came in, opened his mouth and then closed it without saying anything. He bobbed his head down in a quick nod and then looked away.

"Mr. Shane," said Officer Wilton, indicating the chair next to Hank.

"If it's all the same," I said, "I think I'd rather sit here."

I pulled out a chair and sat down on the end of the table, out of Hank's reach.

"That's fine," said Wilton and took a seat himself.

I waited while he shuffled a handful of papers until he found what he was looking for.

"Mr. Ingram has made a statement about what happened in Room 107. Since you were in the room at the time, I want to ask you to listen to this statement and tell me if it accords with what you saw and heard."

I looked at Hank.

"Is this okay, Hank? Does he have your permission?"

Hank closed his eyes but nodded.

Wilton spoke carefully and with great courtesy.

"This is not an official investigation, Mr. Shane. I will have to report the incident, of course, and what happens after that, I do not know. At the moment, that doesn't concern me and it need not concern you. I assured Mr. Ingram and I assure you that at this point, we are just trying to sort out what happened. Mr. Ingram had a permit to carry the weapon. What I need to know is whether you corroborate his story."

"Should I have an attorney present?" I asked, not sure what authority Wilton had and how my words might get twisted later if there were some sort of lawsuit.

"No need, whatsoever," Wilton assured me.

I pulled out my cell phone and tapped a record app.

"Do you mind, then, if I at least keep a record of what I say? Just in case I need proof later."

He sighed.

"You can record anything you want. Lord knows, people record things all the time on those damn phones without asking anyone's permission. Go ahead, if it will make you feel better. But I promise you, there is no reason to do so."

"I think I will, though, all the same," I said and placed the phone on the table between me and the officer.

He looked at the phone, at me and then at Hank.

"Mr. Ingram, do you agree to allow Mr. Shane to record this? After all, this is your statement."

Hank wiped a hand across his forehead and thought for a moment.

"What the heck. You've got it in writing already."

He turned to me with a pleading look on his face.

"But Corny, for old time's sake, for the sake of our kids, for God's sake, promise me you won't share that recording with anyone else without letting me know first."

For old time's sake.

"Hank, that is your private matter. Tell you what. I won't record the reading of the statement. I'll turn this off," and I tapped the app to close it, "until I start talking after hearing the statement. All I want is a record of what I say. How does that sound? Fair enough?"

He let out a long breath.

"Yeah, fair enough. Thanks. I knew … I knew I could trust you," he said under his breath.

"Hank," my voice broke, "you can trust me. What's past is past and …"

Officer Wilton cleared his throat and broke in.

"I gather, gentlemen, that you have things to talk about other than what happened here tonight. Right now I need us all to focus, however, on the events in Room 107. Feel free to have a little *tête-à-tête* later on your own time."

"*Tête-à-tête*, Officer Witlton?" I couldn't resist saying, "you interest me strangely."

He grinned and blushed.

"My kid gave me one of those calendars with a new word every day. She said I needed to class up my act so I don't embarrass her sounding like the redneck I am."

Hank and I looked at one another and chuckled.

"Yeah, we've got kids. Been there, done that!"

He straightened his papers.

"Seriously though, it's 2:30 in the morning and I'm sure y'all want to get home. It's up to you. I have to be here all night."

"Read on," I said.

Given how long Wilton had been talking with Hank, the statement itself was fairly brief. I listened carefully and at the end nodded my head. I reached over and tapped the phone app and checked to make sure it was working.

"Testing testing one two three."

I tapped it again and my voice came back at me with that unfamiliar tone that my recorded voice always has: "Testing testing one two three."

Satisfied, I put the phone on the table and began.

"Crazy as that must sound, it's what I remember. I mean, I don't know about what Hank thought or what he said to Chanice out in the hall or anything like that. You'll just have to take his word for that. But," I looked directly at Hank, "I can say I trust him to be telling you the truth as best he can."

Wilton shook his head.

"So you say this winged guy came through the window and touched Mr. Ingram's son?"

"Yes. As Mr. Ingram told you, my daughter and I had come to the hospital because she wanted to tell Hank, Jr. – that's Mr. Ingram's son – that she was sorry about him getting hurt. Mr. and Mrs. Ingram agreed to give her a minute and they left the room so that she could have some privacy. I stayed with her while they waited out in the hall. The door was open so they could see in, but they were good enough to give step away so that they couldn't hear anything."

Wilton nodded.

"Anyway, Katie, that's my daughter, she went over and had just started talking to Hank, Jr. when I heard a rap on the window. I looked over, thinking it might just be a tree limb or something in the wind. But then I saw Angelo …"

Wilton looked down at his papers.

"Who's Angelo?"

"Angelo is the boy with the wings. At least, that's what Katie calls him. He doesn't talk, so she doesn't really know his name."

Wilton made a note on a separate sheet of paper and looked up.

"Is he Mexican, with a name like Angelo?"

I leaned back in my chair.

"We … I don't know if he's Mexican or what he is. And Angelo may not be his name. That's just what Katie calls him."

"Does he look Mexican? I know the police are going to want a description of this guy, disappearing like he did."

I thought for a moment and looked at Hank. He shrugged his shoulders.

"I don't think he looked particularly Mexican. Except for his wings, he looked like any other kid around here."

I remember when Katie had said something like that. *Except for his wings*.

"Okay," Wilton said, "so you saw this kid flapping his wings and knocking on the window. Then what? Mr. Ingram wasn't there, so he didn't tell me any of this stuff."

"Katie yelled something, his name, I think. You know, 'Angelo!' or something and went over to the window."

Hank butted in.

"That was when I started for the room. I didn't see what was going on, but I saw her leave Hank's bed and I wondered what was up."

I continued.

"Katie opened the window and Angelo came in."

Wilton was making more notes.

"And what were you doing?"

"I was just standing there. The whole thing was so strange and … I just stood there. Angelo came in, like I said, and I wondered how he got those big wings through the narrow window opening."

I turned to Hank.

"You know how sometimes when something happens, something like an accident, and your mind focuses on an extraneous detail? A detail that isn't all that important, but it's like your mind can't take in what's happening and so it tries to fix on something it can handle."

Hank nodded and I turned back to Wilton.

"So I stood there wondering how he got those big white wings through the window. And he and Katie walked over to Hank's bed. I may have said something, I don't know. Like 'Don't touch him' or 'Stop.' I wouldn't swear to that. It all happened fast. Then Angelo put his hand on Hank's head and then things got crazy."

I glanced at Hank, Sr.

"That's when he came in and the machines were blinking and Hank, Jr. opened his eyes and there was a gun shot, no, two gunshots, and the window exploded and Katie fell and … Well, the rest of it is in that statement."

Wilton looked from me to Hank and back at me.

"And when did the guy with the wings leave? And how? Mr. Ingram says he didn't notice. Did you?"

I shook my head.

"I didn't see anything. I was so worried about Katie, she was bleeding ..."

Hank's head jerked around and I put out a hand toward him.

"No, she wasn't bleeding. I thought she was bleeding because I saw blood. Or what I thought was blood. But the nurse told me that when they cleaned Katie up, she didn't have any scratches from the broken glass. No wounds at all. And certainly," I said firmly, "not from any bullet."

Hank sank back and whispered, "Oh, thank God!"

I looked at him and said, "And Hank didn't have any wounds either."

"The nurse also told me," I said, turning back to Wilton, "that they found no sign of Angelo in the room when they were cleaning up. The custodial staff swept and mopped glass, moved furniture around, checked the closet and bathroom. No Angelo. I guess he just flew off."

Wilton looked at me.

"He. Just. Flew. Off."

"I guess. I mean, he got in through that window and he must have gone out that window."

"And nobody saw this?"

Hank shook his head, I shook my head, Wilton shook his head and made another note on his pad.

I almost said, "Maybe Katie saw him," but caught myself. I didn't want anyone waking Katie up in the middle of the night, not after all she had been through. I could ask her myself the next morning.

"What about Hank, Jr." I said instead.

"What about him?" Wilton and Hank said simultaneously.

"He was awake by then. And he was looking around the room. He looked right at Angelo for a second. Maybe he saw something."

Hank half rose from his chair.

"You are not going to bother that boy …"

Wilton waved him back.

"Don't worry. There's plenty of time. Doctor Weller already told me that they put your son in ICU and those nurses won't let me within a mile of him until the doctors say they can."

He looked at the clock on the wall. It was well past three o'clock.

"I guess that's all for now. Like I say, this is not a formal investigation, not the police or anything. But I will have to file a report and you may be hearing from someone in a more official capacity soon. As far as I can tell, no one got hurt, unless it was the guy with the wings and heck if I know where he is anyway. Y'all can go. But" he said in his best cop voice, "don't leave town."

Chapter 27

Hank and I walked out into the waiting area and stood there silent. Then we both spoke at the same time.

"I'm …"

"I'm …"

We stopped and laughed awkwardly.

"You first," I said.

"I'm so sorry about all this," he said simply.

I held out my hand.

"I am the one who is sorry, Hank, about everything. I really am. I wasn't putting on when I said that stuff in the room. I know I wrecked everything and I know there are things I can't undo."

He sighed heavily.

"Things like this put a lot of crap in perspective, though, don't they? I thought my son was going to die. And then I thought I had shot your daughter. Corny, Corny, how did it come to this? How did we come to this?"

He stared at his feet and I put my hands on his shoulders.

"I don't know. It's all crazy. But the main thing is, Hank, Jr. is okay, Katie's okay. And we, maybe we can work on being okay?"

He sighed again and looked up.

"I can try," he said."

"Well, I could use a ride home," I said, only half kidding. I didn't have my bike with me.

"Sure," he said, "I think we can start with that. Remember all those times we drove around and around in our parents' cars, talking about what we were going to do?"

We headed toward the door when I came to a sudden stop.

"Hank, where's Chanice?"

"Crap!" he shouted and headed over to the main desk.

As he did so, Chanice came around the corner with Dr. Weller.

"Hank!" she called, relief and exhaustion both evident in her voice.

He walked over and I drifted close enough to hear.

Doctor Weller explained that they had been examining Hank, Jr. All tests indicated that he was fine, he was alert and relaxed and asking for his parents.

Chanice had spent several agitated hours in the intensive care unit's waiting area, afraid to believe everything was okay. When the doctors finally came to get her, she said she nearly fell over. When she heard the news, she began to cry and Dawneen Philips had come to help her. After the first storm of happy tears were over, she thought to ask about Hank, Sr.

"That security man took him away. Where is he? He needs to know Hank, Jr. is okay. Where is he? They didn't … they didn't arrest him did they? He's not in jail! All he was doing was trying to protect our boy. They wouldn't put him in jail for that, would they? Not for defending his own son?"

Dawneen promised to find out what had happened to Hank and got Chanice a cup of tea to sip while she phoned around. Five minutes later she was back with the news that Hank, Sr. was not in jail, had not been arrested and in fact had just been released to go home.

Chanice clutched her overnight-bag-sized purse and struggled to her feet.

"I have to find him. He's probably looking for me so we can go home."

Doctor Weller offered to take her to find Hank and now they were all gathered in the lobby. When Chanice told Hank that she had been afraid he was worried about her and wandering all over the hospital looking for her, he glanced and me and I smiled, putting a my right index finger over my lips. No need for Chanice to know he had forgotten she was even there.

Doctor Weller cleared his throat and flipped open a chart he had been carrying under his arm.

"Well, Mr. and Mrs. Ingram," he said calmly, "your boy had a bad time of it but he is doing great right now. That's the way it is with some of these comas. Sometimes people just pop out of them like nothing happened. You recall we told you that might happen and it turns out that we were right."

"But what happened?" Chanice demanded. "Did that boy who was in there do something? Some kind of miracle?"

The doctor frowned.

"What boy?"

"The boy with the wings," she said. "The boy who came through the window and laid his hands on Hank, just like in the Bible."

Doctor Weller apparently had not heard this part of the story, nor was he inclined to give it much credence. He looked at Hank, Sr. and grinned. I could see the thought run through his mind: *Women, what are you gonna do?* His response to Chanice, however, was courteous, although he was not able to keep a note of amusement out of his deep voice.

"No need to drag miracles into it, Mrs. Ingram. Like I said, this happens sometime. The body has resources that we don't always understand and we can't always predict what will happen. But it's all perfectly natural. Sometimes people who have been in comas for much longer than Hank, Jr, months or even years, wake up like they had just fallen asleep."

"Can we see him?" she asked.

"I think I can let you and Mr. Ingram look in for just a moment. But he has had quite a night and you must both be exhausted. So one minute. Then you go home and get some rest. Come back this afternoon. We will keep him under observation and I wouldn't be surprised if we release him and let him go home this evening."

Chanice clung to Hank and began to cry.

"Oh, thank you, Jesus!" she said over and over. "Thank you! Thank you! Thank you!"

Hank wrapped an arm around her and said to the doctor, "And thank you Dr. Weller. And all the staff. This has been such a trial for Chanice and me and really for all of us."

Docotor Weller nodded, closed the file chart and offered to take them back to Intensive Care and assure the nurses that they had permission to see Hank, Jr. for one minute.

"One minute," he repeated, looking at Chanice.

Hank looked at me.

"I'll find another way home," I said. "I'll call you later."

"No, wait. Doctor," Hank said, "can my friend come, too? He's not family but … Can he come, too?"

Doctor Weller frowned.

"Intensive Care is not set up for a lot of visitors. And we don't want to excite the patient with a crowd."

He looked at me.

"Do you mind?"

I shook my head vigorously.

"No, I understand. I told you, Hank, I'll find a way home. We can talk tomorrow."

He looked undecided but Chanice was tugging at him. She wanted to see her son and she wanted to see him now.

"Wait here," Hank told me. "I said I would give you a ride home and I will. After all, they're only going to let us have a minute," he grinned at Doctor Weller, "one minute. We'll be right back."

I agreed and went back to the waiting area.

Doctor Weller was not joking about only giving them one minute. I had just gotten comfortable in a chair, leaned back and closed my eyes when Hank's voice rang in my ears.

"Wake up, sleepy head. Time to go."

He and Chanice both looked tired, but it was no longer tiredness tinged with fear and anxiety. You know how they say people age in just a few hours in times of stress? Hank and Chanice had aged a lot that night, but now their relaxed faces made them look more like the young folks I had once known.

I could tell Chanice was surprised that Hank and I were on speaking terms. She gave me a strange look when we got to Hank' SUV, but she didn't ask any questions. Once Hank started the car up, she began to babble about what had happened and kept it up until Hank pulled up into my driveway. The gist of her jibber-jabber was that it had been a miracle, no matter what that Doctor Weller thought, that she had seen it herself and that boy with the wings was obviously an angel sent by Jesus in answer to a mother's prayers. Didn't we see how the room filled with light when he came in, and he must have just walked right through the walls or flown through the windows. How else did he get there with those big white wings? It was a miracle, that's what it was. She was going to tell everybody and no one was going to tell her different.

I thanked Hank and promised to talk to him later.

"I'll give y'all a chance to get some sleep. Lord knows, I need some myself. But I'll call late in the afternoon to see if they're going to let Hank, Jr go home. And if you need anything, anything at all, you call me. Y'hear?"

Hank nodded. As I closed the door, I heard Chanice saying, "I should call one of those television stations in Austin, no, in Dallas or Houston. This is big news, big news!"

Hank was shaking his head as the SUV backed out of my drive and pulled away.

Chapter 28

The house looked dark except for the porch lights in front and back. I opened the front door and slipped inside. I took off my boots and left them beside the door, walking as softly as I could so as not to disturb Miss Missouri, Katie or Billy Bob. According to my phone, it was 4:15.

The door to the kids' room was ajar and I peeked inside. By the glow of a nightlight, I could see Miss Missouri and Katie asleep in Katie's princess bed. The bed was shaped like Cinderella's pumpkin carriage, pink and lavender and as girly as could be. It was barely big enough for the two of them, but after the night they had had, I am sure they fell asleep easily. I tiptoed over and looked down at Billy Bob. His pacifier had fallen out of his mouth and his chest moved gently. He was so beautiful to me in that moment, and my heart ached to think something bad might ever happen to him. I leaned over and kissed the top of his head. He shifted but didn't wake.

When I turned to tiptoe out, I saw Miss Missouri's eyes were open. I put my finger over my mouth and said, "Everything is okay. Everything. Go back to sleep."

I put my hands together and leaned my head against them.

She smiled, said, "Good," and closed her eyes.

I made my way to my own bedroom and fell on top of the bed, still in my jeans and t-shirt. Just before I fell asleep, I remembered Wayne's advice and looked at the ceiling.

"Thank you," I said. And I really meant it.

I don't know when the others woke up. The Texas sun was streaming through my west-facing window when I finally opened my eyes. For a split second, I wondered if it had all been a dream. The boy with the wings, Hank, Jr. hurting himself, Hank, Sr. shooting out the hospital window. Chanice talking about calling the television news.

I lay there for a minute or two and then I heard Miss Missouri and Katie talking down the hall. I rolled over and got out of bed. I looked around for my boots and it took a minute or two before I remembered leaving them by the front door when I came in after Hank dropped me off. I had a flashback to the many times Hank had dropped me off at my parents' house in the wee hours and I had taken my boots off and tiptoed in my stocking feet past their bedroom. I grinned and looked down at my socks, wiggling my toes.

I checked my phone and saw that it was almost four and that there were no messages. I sniffed under my arms, decided I could postpone showering until later and wandered down the kitchen to get something to eat. Suddenly I felt famished.

Miss Missouri and Katie were in the kitchen.

"Look, Daddy's up," Katie announced, looking up from a bowl filled with some thick brown batter. "Miss Missouri's teaching me how to make fudge. Do you want pecans in it or not?"

"How can you ask? We are the original pecan people! The more, the nuttier; the nuttier, the better."

Miss Missouri watched Katie start to pour chopped pecans into the batter and warned her, "Not too many, now! Fold them in the way I showed you. If you dump them all at once, it will be hard to mix and you won't have fudge, you'll just have a messy bowl of goop."

Katie nodded and folded pecan meats into the fudge with a spatula that was white with black markings like a cowhide.

"Now pour it into the pan before it sets up," Missouri told her.

Katie struggled with the mixing bowl and I came to her rescue.

"I'll hold it and you scrape the fudge out," I suggested.

"Thanks," she said.

When she finished she held the spatula up and looked at me.

"You want to lick this or can I?"

I was really hungry but my fatherly instincts kicked in.

"You can have that. I think I need something for my late breakfast that is not quite so much sugar."

"Miss Missouri?" Katie asked politely, holding out the spatula to our neighbor.

"It's all yours, sweetie," the old lady said. "Can I get you something for breakfast, Corny? I would say brunch but it's way past lunch. Brupper? Breakfast and supper?"

"Brupper? I don't think so. That sounds totally unappetizing," I said. "I can manage."

I got two breakfast sandwiches out of the freezer, unwrapped them and folded them into a paper towel, placed the bundle on a saucer and set it in the microwave to cook.

"How old is this coffee?" I asked, sniffing the inky stuff in the glass pot.

"Almost as old as I am," Missouri said. "I'll make another pot. I think I could use a fresh cup myself."

I got out of her way and went to sit at the table where Katie was finishing up licking her spatula, turning it from side to side, looking for any places she had missed. Finally seeing that there were no morsels left, she lay it down on a paper napkin and looked at me happily.

"Hank's okay," she announced.

"I know," I said, then felt guilty for having robbed her of the pleasure of telling me. "I mean, I was there last night when the doctor told Hank and Chanice. I take it," I turned to Missouri who was watching the coffee pot do its thing, "that he is still okay?"

She nodded.

"Wanda Mae called me to tell me the news is all over town. She said that Chanice is telling everyone it was a miracle, that Jesus sent an angel to cure Hank, Jr. because she had been praying so hard. Sounds to me like she might be trying to get a little credit for the miracle, if it was a miracle, which I don't for a minute believe."

I feigned shock.

"Why, Missouri Venables, do you mean to stand there and tell me that you, a fine Christian woman, don't believe in miracles."

She sniffed.

"Of course, I believe in miracles. The Bible is full of them. But the age of miracles is over. It ended when the last apostle died. In the beginning," she said pedantically, "God worked miracles through the apostles so people would believe the good news about Jesus. But after the apostles died, people had to start believing on the testimony of Christians and not on showy things like magic."

I nodded, although her logic seemed to have at least one major hole in it. But I was not in a mood to argue religion. I was more interested in hearing about our local good news.

"So Hank, Jr. is okay. Doctor Weller," I told them, "said they might even let him go home today. I'll have to check with Hank later and see if that's the case."

Miss Missouri and Katie both looked at me.

"Check with Hank," Miss Missouri said.

"Yeah, we … well, we talked after everything happened. I won't say we got it all straightened out. I won't say we will get it all straightened out. A lot of water has flowed under the bridge, a lot of tears since all that stuff happened. But anyway, we're talking. He even gave me a ride home last night."

Missouri looked at Katie.

"Okay, now that might be a miracle," she said with a smile.

"And speaking of miracles, Doctor Weller didn't seem to be buying Chanice's story about any miracle. He said things like this happen sometimes with coma victims, that people who have been out a lot longer than Hank, Jr. come around. They're not sure what happened in this case, but there's no need to get all hopped up about miracles."

"Hmmm," Miss Missouri said.

"What?" I asked. "That was a pregnant *hmmm*."

She turned pink and turned around to get the coffee. She poured me a cup and then one for herself and sat down before answering me.

"I talked to Dawneen a little while ago, just to check up on what Wanda Mae said. Wanda Mae doesn't always get her facts straight. She has a tendency to hear what she wants to hear and when she repeats things, she can't help making it sound more interesting that it is. Anyway, Dawneen said that it's true. Hank is okay. I told her what Chanice was saying and she laughed. 'That's Chanice if ever anything was. She just wants to be the center of attention.' I told her that was what I thought, and then she told me what you just said Doc Weller said, that things like this happen with comas sometime. But she did say there was one odd thing."

"What was that?"

"Well, she said Hank not only came out of the coma, but when they ran the tests and checked him out, they found no sign of trauma, his bruises had disappeared and a couple of bad scratches had healed completely. Not even a scar to show where they had been."

Katie nodded.

"It was a miracle. Angelo touched him and he got well. Just like that. I knew it."

I took a deep drink of my coffee before responding.

"Well, miracle is a fancy word, it seems to me, for something we don't understand but that we are happy about. I am willing to call this a miracle in that sense. I don't understand it, I don't know what happens to coma people, I sure don't know why Hank's bruises and scratches disappeared. But I know one thing for sure. It makes me happy and that's enough.

I looked at Miss Missouri.

"Wayne told me something that I think fits this situation. Someone asked him once how AA works. How was it supposed to help people keep sober. What was the gimmick, the trick. 'I just told him, you want to know how it works? I'll tell you. It works just fine.'"

Chapter 29

And that's about all there is to tell.

We never saw Angelo again. Neither Hank nor Katie saw him leave the room and no one but those of us who had been there had seen him at all. I guess he went back to wherever it was he came from to begin with. Katie talked about him for a long time and then she started to talk about other boys. Boys without wings.

Miss Missouri drove us over to Austin and I bought Katie some of the clothes she wanted. Not all of them. She was growing up faster than I wanted as it was.

Somehow Hank talked Chanice out of taking her miracle story to the news people, but that didn't keep her from spreading it all over Blakesfield. She and Joanne Smithers had the town divided for a while over whether Angelo was a devil or an angel, but eventually everyone got tired of the argument. Joanne married a preacher from Davis who did not believe women should speak in church, and that was the last I ever heard about her.

LuNella came back to visit a few times, but she never came back to stay. She had found her new life in Ponca City.

As for me, I never could make up my mind about Angelo. I told Wayne, though, that I thought I had found my higher power. He may have just been a kid, and he never said a word. But he did have wings, and that ought to count for something.

Chapter 30

Oh, I guess there is one more thing to tell. That happened some years later.

Chapter 31

I stood at the back of the Blakesfield Bible Baptist Church. Sunlight streamed through the frosted glass panels in the windows and illuminated the flowers that flanked the altar. The pews were filling as a few people still straggled in. The organist was playing unfamiliar hymns, alternating with classical music. A harpist was seated behind her, hands plucking at air as she practiced something in her head.

Behind me I heard rustles and turned to look at the bride.

Katie was as beautiful as her mother had been at that age. I don't know how to describe the dress she wore. It looked pretty much like every bridal gown I had ever seen. I know that it had cost a small fortune that LuNella and her husband had insisted on paying. The women had chattered about lace panels and other things that flew over my head, something about seed pearls and Irish nuns. Or was in Belgian nuns? It didn't matter. It fit Katie perfectly and she shone brighter than the sun coming through the windows.

The woman who was in charge of the ceremony waved me over.

"Now, Mr. Shane, you and the bride stand back here while I get the rest of the wedding party lined up."

She guided me into place in the back of the foyer, next to Katie. She shifted me into place on Katie's right.

"Isn't she beautiful?" the woman whispered and squeezed my arm.

"You are," I said to Katie.

"Thanks, Daddy," she whispered.

She looked at me and said, "Are you nervous?"

I shook my head.

"No, not at all," I lied through my teeth.

She smiled and put her hand out to still my right hand. I was holding my brass ten-year coin and rubbing it between my thumb and forefinger.

"You're going to rub that thing smooth if you aren't careful."

I made a wry smile and slipped the coin into the pocket of my black suit coat.

"It helps keep me calm, I guess," I admitted.

"We'll be fine."

The organ had stopped and there was a brief silence. The doors into the sanctuary were closed and the lady gave us final directions.

"Okay, everyone," she said, showing her teeth, "big smiles."

She looked around and seemed satisfied.

"Remember, let the person in front of you get two pews ahead before you start. And step, step, step."

She opened the doors. The pastor, groom and best man came from a side door at the front and positioned themselves. They turned and faced the rear of the church. The pastor caught the eye of the harpist and nodded. The first notes of Pachelbel's "Canon in D" floated back and the director sent the three bridesmaids in their pale yellow gowns down, one after the other, two pews spaced between them. Then Belinda, Katie's BFF and maid of honor, beaming and nodding from side to side like the day was all about her.

LuNella was seated in the front row reserved for the family of the bride. Beside her sat her husband, Amos Gates, a math teacher she had met in Ponca City. The typewriter repairman was long gone and happily forgotten.

Chanice sat alone in her pew on the opposite side of the aisle. Neither she nor Hank had remarried after they split up, and they seemed to have a very successful divorce. They had even become friends in the aftermath of their failed marriage.

I knew that Chanice was dating Wayne, but she had mentioned that she wasn't going to bring him to the wedding. He was there as Katie's guest, sitting on bride's side in the back row. He told her he wouldn't miss it for the world, but he also claimed that he had to get back to work as soon as the ceremony was over and would miss the reception.

LuNella had told me privately that Chanice and Wayne thought this would be for the best.

"No need for anyone to pay any attention to me," Chanice told LuNella. "This day is for our kids. They don't need any parental drama getting in the way."

The director sent two little flower girls down the aisle, scattering yellow rose petals. My brother Richard's youngest, Wade, followed with the ring on a lacy pillow. His parents beamed from their place up front and my sister-in-law took picture after picture on her phone.

Finally it was our turn. The harpist segued into Wagner's "Bridal Chorus" and the guests rose to their feet and turned to look. The director gestured for us to start the long march. Katie slipped her hand under my left arm, and moved slowly through the door. I kept pace. Belinda had looked from side to side, greeting people with a smile. I had eyes only for Katie, and she had eyes only for her groom.

Hank, Jr. stood tall and straight, looking solemn but happy. His father, his best man, stood beside him. He had joked with me beforehand that he was there to make sure his son didn't fall over in a dead faint or break into a dead run. Billy Bob was there, too, among the groomsmen. He had promised Hank, Sr. that he would help hold Hank, Jr. down if he tried to do a bunk.

When Katie and I reached the steps of the sanctuary, I kissed her and gave her hand to Hank, Jr. As I turned to go to the pew to sit beside LuNella and her husband, Hank, Sr. caught my eye, grinned and winked.

We had come a long way, I thought. Twenty-five years before, Hank and LuNella and I had planned another wedding, one that was destined never to be. Now we were here together, unexpectedly witnessing the wedding of our children. And we were doing it as friends.

Miss Missouri's face flashed through my mind for a second. She had died three years before.

"If you could see us now, Miss Missouri," I said, tearing up.

LuNella must have heard me. She leaned toward me and whispered, "She probably can, you know."

I didn't really believe that, not the way LuNella meant it. But it was a nice idea. I nodded at her, reached into my pocket and rubbed my ten-year coin.

Baptist weddings don't take long. It seemed just a minute later Hank, Jr. was lifting Katie's veil and kissing her. Only then did I notice that there were small white feathers woven into the crown of roses in her hair.

People applauded and I think I heard a cheer or two from the back where the groom's buddies sat, punching one another in the arm and congratulating themselves on still being free.

The organist struck up something traditional and the newlyweds waited for the ushers to lead the families and friends outside, where other friends handed out small net bags filled with white confetti and tied with white ribbons. Finally Katie and Hank came through the doors and cheers erupted again as confetti filled the air. Some of it landed on my sleeve, and as I shook it off, I noticed that the small bits of paper were not cut into squares or circles or hearts. Each one was a tiny white feather. I looked sharply at Katie, but she was facing the other direction.

The couple walked down the steps to a waiting limousine that would take them to the reception at the club. As Hank held the door for his bride, I saw her look up and pause.

I could swear I heard the sound of wings, but when I looked up into the sun, I didn't see anything.

Katie caught my eye and smiled crookedly, raising an eyebrow.

She held out her hand to help Hank into the limo and they rode away.

Made in the USA
Charleston, SC
24 May 2016